A Rose by Any Other Name

by

Alana Lorens

This is a work of fiction. Names, characters, places, and incidents are either the product of the author's imagination or are used fictitiously, and any resemblance to actual persons living or dead, business establishments, events, or locales, is entirely coincidental.

A Rose by Any Other Name

COPYRIGHT © 2022 by Barbara J Mountjoy

Cover Art by *Kristian Norris*

The Wild Rose Press, Inc.
PO Box 708
Adams Basin, NY 14410-0708
Visit us at www.thewildrosepress.com

Publishing History
First Edition, 2022
Trade Paperback ISBN 978-1-5092-3929-0
Digital ISBN 978-1-5092-3930-6

Published in the United States of America

Reconnecting with her high school buds did hold some appeal. Teresa and Analisa had pulled Marisol through some pretty rough times, including the death of her mother. She'd done the same for them, the three of them spending many of their darkest nights supporting each other like the sisters none of them had. They stayed in touch a few times a year, just enough to make sure nothing terrible had happened.

Sure would be nice to see them again in person.

Listening to the keening sound of insects in the palm trees overhead, she leaned back and closed her eyes. Maybe she could do it.

None of them knew she was Jerrika Jones. She carefully protected her identity—or more correctly, her son's identity—over the last dozen years while she built her brand as the single mothers' go-to girl. Hard as it was to score points with a teenaged son, she'd decided not to task him with the potential embarrassment of a hopefully-famous-someday mother as well.

But now that Mark got out on his own more, maybe she could claim her sassy online personality. She could show West Exeter that the girl voted most likely to work as an invisible clerical made something of herself after all. All on her own.

More energized, she went inside, washed her face, and clicked the email. Many of the activities listed were too fancy for her limited budget. The '80s-themed dance caught her eye. She smiled at the thought of all of them back in Madonna-esque lace gloves, hair ratted up as high as they could get it to stand, bangs looking like a tidal wave, dancing to Blondie's "Heart of Glass" or Wham!'s "Wake Me Up Before You Go-Go."

Just maybe, this moment could change her life.

Other Wild Rose Press Titles by Alana Lorens

Conviction of the Heart
Secrets in the Sand
Tender Misdemeanors
That Girl's the One I Love
Voodoo Dreams

Dedication

For all those who have lost a love…
and found them again

Acknowledgments:

A special thanks to my Wild Rose editor Ally Robertson for her constant support and dedication to helping me put out the best books ever!

Chapter One

And so, another victory for Woman on her own.

Jerrika Jones gave her blog post a quick once-over for typos and hit "publish." As the words appeared on her Web site, she quipped aloud, "Another successful message from one of America's up-and-coming mommy bloggers, brought to you by Anatole Pasta and Juicy Trees baby food."

Satisfaction eluded her, despite meeting her deadline. Some days, she felt like she just turned out copy, mostly words, no heart or soul. After surviving not only the end of the world—as everyone called the big computer transition from 1999 to 2000—but four years writing the *Mothering Without a Man* blog, she typed on autopilot more and more frequently.

"Does Heather Armstrong ever feel like this? Please, *Dios mio*, tell me she does."

At least the sponsors she had gradually attracted were finally starting to pay her bills. She didn't live plush, but she had what she needed.

Annoyed at talking to herself, she turned to the shelf behind her to pop another coffee pack into the new coffee brewer, received as a gift from a sponsor. She never made a full pot anymore. If she made it, she drank it. If she drank it, she would find herself a nervous wreck by bedtime. Ever since she passed forty, caffeine hit her like speed.

She wouldn't have to talk to herself if Mark ever hung out at home, their small two-bedroom apartment in downtown Ocala. He might not stay around much, but her son was a good boy, studied hard, and worked an after-school job to pay for his own car and insurance. He also found cash and time to entertain Kiko Suarez, his wonderful steady girlfriend. He had his reasons for being absent, especially now in his senior year.

Two months till he graduated. Jerrika could afford to be patient. She'd worked hard to raise that boy all by herself.

The small jungle bird sound signifying the arrival of new email went off, and she glanced up at the screen in front of her. The mail wasn't for Jerrika Jones, the snappy woman moving up to the B list of the blogging community, the one with a Technorati rating in the 300s. It came addressed to Marisol Herrera Slade.

She removed her metaphorical blogger's hat and settled back into her natural persona. Marisol, not Jerrika, was the one struggling to find a way to pay for Mark's tuition at Florida State University, where he wanted to study computer forensics. Probably another letter asking for fee money, money Marisol didn't possess. She hitched up imaginary bootstraps and opened the mail.

It announced her twentieth high school reunion. Had it been that many years since she'd graduated from George F. Wright High School? *Now it was 2004...yeah. That was just about right.*

Not what she expected at all. She blinked and read the email again, a letter from Debbie Emerson Vogan. Marisol remembered Debbie—the petite blonde always in charge of every organization, not because she wanted the popularity, but because she excelled at it. Her cute little smile didn't hurt, either.

But a reunion? *No way.* Twenty years she'd spent putting miles between herself and that horrid high school experience in the small town of West Exeter, Pennsylvania. She'd never been particularly good at anything but her English classes, where she'd begun the writing style that still carried her today. Memories still burned, the worst ones of Russell Asher, the boy she was sure was The One. They'd dated for half a year before he'd dumped Marisol.

His Black mother and his white father's relationship represented the optimism of the late 1960s and the Age of Aquarius. They proved a mixed marriage could work. But Russell was a sports star, with all the ego-induced quirks that came along with that status. He was determined to be "somebody." Marisol, the daughter of former migrant workers, apparently didn't measure up to Tiffany Kearns, the pretty golden girl cheerleader whose rich daddy owned the car dealerships and the fancy house on Lake Pymatuning. So Marisol ran away. She never returned either.

Unresolved feelings about Russell drove her up out of her chair. She must *do* something, right now. *Get some air.* She grabbed the well-worn red plastic watering can from behind the back door and stepped out onto her patio.

In perfect honesty, the collection of clay and ceramic pots rimming her back door didn't actually form a "patio." The eight square feet simply housed a dozen large plants and a couple of folding chairs. The pots contained a multihued, vivid collection of tropical flora: red and yellow crotons, bright pink hibiscus, a small purple bougainvillea, assorted coleus, and several aromatic cooking herbs.

The late April sun warmed her bare shoulders as she moved around the small area, watering each plant just a little, more to occupy her hands than because they needed it. Here in Ocala, Florida, they called Easter to Halloween the monsoon season, as it probably rained at some point nearly every day. One of these days, she hoped to find a used patio umbrella at a thrift store. She'd put it up over her folding chair so she could even sit out in the rain if she wanted to. Better than spending all day in her tiny apartment, hunched over her keyboard.

But she couldn't forget that email.

Did she really want to see all those people again? What would they say if they saw her?

What if they knew I am Jerrika Jones?

She opened her chair and sat down, pensive as she picked the budding seed tops off the coleus.

Reconnecting with her high school buds did hold some appeal. Teresa and Analisa had pulled Marisol through some pretty rough times, including the death of her mother. She'd done the same for them, the three of them spending many of their darkest nights supporting each other like the sisters none of them had. They stayed in touch a few times a year, just enough to make sure nothing terrible had happened.

Sure would be nice to see them again in person.

Listening to the keening sound of insects in the palm trees overhead, she leaned back and closed her eyes. Maybe she could do it.

None of them knew she was Jerrika Jones. She carefully protected her identity—or more correctly, her son's identity—over the last dozen years while she built her brand as the single mothers' go-to girl. Hard as it was to score points with a teenaged son, she'd decided not to task him with the potential embarrassment of a hopefully-famous-someday mother as well.

But now that Mark got out on his own more, maybe she could claim her sassy online personality. She could show West Exeter that the girl voted most likely to work as an invisible clerical made something of herself after all. All on her own.

More energized, she went inside, washed her face, and clicked the email. Many of the activities listed were too fancy for her limited budget. The '80s-themed dance caught her eye. She smiled at the thought of all of them back in Madonna-esque lace gloves, hair ratted up as high as they could get it to stand, bangs looking like a tidal wave, dancing to Blondie's "Heart of Glass" or Wham!'s "Wake Me Up Before You Go-Go."

Just maybe, this moment could change her life.

She could deal with the hurtful memories, even ignore them if she had to.

"Take that, Russell Asher!" she said as she sent her RSVP.

Chapter Two

Russell Asher leaned back in his chair and rubbed his eyes. Too much time in front of the computer the last couple of days. He'd let himself get sucked into some seemingly endless raids on his simulated war MMORPG game, the extent of any military experience he'd had. Usually he played well, but today, the longer he'd played, the worse he'd gotten. Finally he'd just begged off and checked his mail.

First there was a reminder from his dads' support group of a meeting that night. He didn't know if he was up to going, listening to all the other sad fathers complain about their situations, their stingy exes, their bratty kids, their crappy in-laws. His high school buddy Stuart Fry had dragged him along for the first time several months ago, and at first, Rusty had gotten something useful out of it, helpful tips to take to his lawyers and so on. But after a while, it was just so much more of the same old, same old. So many gloomy stories, and none of them made him feel much better.

Still, it was nice to realize that other people understood his experience.

He shoved his chair away from the desk and dragged himself over to the window, trying to get his blood circulating. He looked down at the street three floors below with lackluster interest.

He ought to go for a run, but that would require

him to change into shorts and sneakers. He waited for motivation to smack him "upside the head," as his soft-spoken, Southern-born mother always said. He stretched his arms behind his back until the muscles burned. He sucked in his abdomen, not yet a 'gut.' Still, not the showpiece from back in his basketball glory days.

Ha.

One season of glory, anyway. That last year of high school and the summer after. Best time of his life.

He thought he'd have it all then, with his sports scholarship, a new car his dad bought him, and the daughter of the man who owned several local car dealerships, madly in love with him. She'd had prospects, too, Tiffany did. She planned to study languages at Penn State so she could work at the United Nations as an interpreter. They'd buy a flashy apartment right off Central Park, he'd work on Wall Street, and they'd own everything they wanted.

The plan had worked, too, for the first several years. They'd both graduated from college, right on schedule, and Tiffy's daddy pulled some strings to get that apartment in the city. Within a few years, they had two perfect sons and the perfect life.

Tiffy still had it. All of it.

She'd taken it from him, thanks to her daddy's team of lawyers and a multi-count divorce. He considered himself lucky to get the boys one weekend a month. The oldest, seventeen, his brother two years younger. Both acted seriously disinterested in a father they openly considered a loser for working as a district manager for Evergreen's drug stores in this Cleveland suburb of Kirtland.

Besides, they'd been the lucky recipients of their mother's genetics, both blond and handsome, though they featured his dark eyes, and the perpetual bronzed tan skin color. In their social circle, Tiffy just pretended she hadn't married a man whose mother came from a line of slaves a hundred years before.

Ugh.

His laptop pinged, and he returned to his desk to see what else might distract him. He blinked with curiosity as he read the invitation to his high school reunion. Now there was something he could get behind.

His promotion pended at work, luckily, and the timing couldn't be better. He'd slide into West Exeter on the wings of his corporate honors. His parents would happily host him. He and the other team members would go out and raise some Cain, and he'd show Tiffy he could do just fine without her.

The glory days would reign again.

He allowed a grin. Feeling more confident, more like himself, he headed to the bedroom to change his shoes for that run.

After his three miles and a protein-loaded freezer dinner, he realized that he didn't want to stay home alone all evening. He debated stopping by a bar, but sitting with a bunch of strangers in some dim room, drowning his sorrows, really didn't appeal to him. So, the meeting, it was. He threw on some khakis and a blue polo shirt and headed out to the Methodist church where the fathers gathered every other Tuesday.

The community room of the church was much like the others he'd seen before: a bulletin board with notices for different groups within and without the church, inoffensive beige walls with some kids' art

8

taped up here and there, a concrete floor painted gray. A circle of worn metal folding chairs sat in the middle of the room, the chairs about half-filled by the time he got there. Stuart, his once-golden hair now a dishwater blond with plenty of gray streaks, cut in a mullet style, waved at Rusty from the near side of the circle. He'd dressed casually as well. He was between jobs, as Rusty recalled, and his current issue with his ex was child support. His old job working for the auto plant had vanished when the union-busting owners moved the company out of the country, and the court refused to lower his support.

Rusty grabbed a Styrofoam cup of bad coffee and sat next to his friend.

"You get the invite to the class reunion?" he asked.

"Yeah. You going?" Stuart sipped from his own white cup and shoved his ragged bangs out of his eyes.

"Sure, why not?"

"Right. You're gonna go and give Tiffy the chance to lord it over you in front of our classmates?" Stuart scoffed, then drained his cup. "Thank God Susan moved out west. I can't imagine she'll bother to come."

Rusty frowned. He'd contemplated some evenings hanging with the guys and reliving sports memories, not confronting his ex-wife. "I can be an adult. She won't want to have a 'scene.' She always hated that stuff."

"Uh-huh."

No point in arguing it. Anything was possible. I'll just have to see what happens. Or sneak around all weekend and avoid her. Shouldn't be that hard.

The group leader for the evening called the meeting to order then, and the dozen men settled into seats and turned their attention to the man. He introduced himself as Tim, and shared that he'd been divorced some ten years, and was the father of three girls. Tim invited them all to tell the group their names and something about their situation, as they saw fit.

Rusty simply disclosed his name and left the details of his failures out. *Depressing enough to think about it, much less say it out loud.*

When they'd gone around the circle, Tim threw the floor open for comments. To Rusty's surprise, Stuart stood up and launched a diatribe about some woman's blog he'd been reading earlier that week.

"Yeah, so I was poking around on the Web, looking for some hope, and I ran across this drivel by this bitch, Jerrika Jones. She's some single mother who's just all about how she's raising her son on her own and he doesn't need a dad. All this crap about how wonderful women are and how men suck!"

His face flushed, he went on, "You bet I signed up for her RSS feed. Every time she posts, I just jump right on there and post a rebuttal, pointing out how she and all the other mommies are full of it. Garbage. Sheer garbage."

Several other men nodded. Comments ranged from "Yeah, women are the worst," to "Someone needs to teach that dog some new tricks."

"All right, calm down," Tim said, trying to temper the emotional fire in the room. "We can discuss this calmly, or we'll have to move on."

"Calmly!" Stuart said. "She's advocating that women cut the fathers out. How is that fair?"

Tim fixed his eyes on Stuart, who gradually sank back into his seat.

"No court would allow that to happen," Rusty interjected. "The laws say that both mothers and fathers should have time with the children."

"Really? You're going to wave the flag for the courts, after you got the shaft? After I did? I see my kids maybe twice a year, and you see yours, what? Once a month? Once a quarter? And you only live an hour away?"

Stuart was on a roll now. Rusty recognized the signs, which had been part of his friend's personality since high school. Once he got started on a debate, he was dug in three hundred percent. Nothing would change his mind. Rusty just raised his hands slightly in defeat and sat back to watch the potential carnage.

One of the other men, a conservative Christian who'd ranted in the past, pulled out his Bible and started quoting sections on how women should be submissive to their men, and that the church should enforce the Biblical laws. Others chimed in with dismay that this Jones woman would surely influence other women to take the children and leave their husbands, and perhaps even become lesbians.

Rusty tried not to roll his eyes. *Okay, this hadn't been a good idea. Better to sit in my kitchen alone rather than entertain some of this…this…* He couldn't even think of a word for it. Ridiculousness, perhaps. He concentrated mightily on drinking the rest of his tasteless coffee, keeping his eyes down so no one would engage him.

Suddenly, his cell rang, and they all turned to glare at him. He, on the other hand, took it as a sign of rescue.

"Sorry, sorry," he mumbled, getting to his feet. "I

forgot to silence it. But it's…work, and I've got to take it. Good night, all!"

Backing away toward the door, he tried not to trip over his tired feet. The last thing he heard before he escaped was Stuart vowing that if he ever met up with this woman, he would definitely "teach her a lesson she wouldn't forget."

Chapter Three

Marisol's rented Toyota tooled down Lake Shore
Drive on Thursday afternoon, the view outside the
window triggering a hundred memories. Her mother
had worked at that hardware store at the north end of
town. Marisol remembered long afternoons after school
in the back room waiting for her to finish work, the
smell of oil and cardboard burned into her mind
forever.

Right there, at the corner of Lakeshore and Third,
Ted LaMonica had gotten fresh on a date in tenth grade,
prompting her to bail out of his Camaro and walk five
miles home. Ghost echoes of the blisters inflicted on
her feet that night tingled as she pressed down on the
accelerator.

Her stomach twisted as she passed the car
dealership Tiffany Kearns' father owned. She'd heard
through the grapevine Russell had stayed with Tiffany
even after college, and they'd gotten married.
Considering how much money Tiffany's dad Gordon
Kearns netted, Marisol pictured the couple as probably
very comfortable.

Sometimes money did buy happiness, didn't it?
Not that I'd know. Not yet. But I'm getting there.

The nagging reminder of Russell persisted as she
drove past the stately white brick mansions on the south
side of town. Did he and blonde Tiffany live in one of

them, bringing up a houseful of pretty mostly-white children with their own trust accounts? She considered the possibility of discovering their address so she could torture herself some more by driving past, just to see their exalted life in play.

Ridiculous.

Her burning face reinforced her good choice in dropping Mark at her father's house in Mercer before she drove out to the lake. Papa happily agreed to host the grandson he'd hardly gotten to know over the years. Mark, on the other hand—less than thrilled—took his cell and his laptop, so hopefully he'd survive the weekend. Probably not without fishing with his grandfather. Papa believed any lesson in life could be best taught with a worm in hand.

Chuckling as she remembered her own sessions in that regard, Marisol turned west on Main Street and headed out to the less-glamorous side of town, where her high-school friend Analisa Ramirez worked as a nurse at the hospital. Still living in the house her parents had owned, she'd invited Marisol to stay with her, like a sleepover from the old days.

The old days, they sure were. Fortuitously, Marisol printed directions off the map-search program on the Internet before she left home, because she'd definitely forgotten how to get there. With unfamiliar roads and changed landmarks, she admitted to herself that things certainly wouldn't stay the same, not more than twenty years.

Some things did not change though. As she continued west, she watched the familiar slow decline in fancy landscaped gardens and straight, unmarred sidewalks morph into increasingly shabby lawns and decrepit cars parked along the street. Indeed, the town's class distinctions remained intact.

She finally pulled into the concrete driveway of Analisa's small two-bedroom brick house at about two o'clock on Thursday afternoon and beeped her horn. Only some purple clematis climbing an arched trellis over the door showed that her friend spent any time in the yard at all.

Analisa came running out—at least she thought she recognized Analisa. The round and curvy woman who emerged from the Ramirez house wore her dark brown hair graying at the temples and pixie-cut short. She sported a brightly-colored print smock and pastel scrub pants, along with white Oxfords and a pearly smile nearly splitting her face.

"*Hola, chica! ¿Que tal?*"

Analisa, practically jumping up and down, held her arms open as Marisol climbed out of the car. As soon as her friend came within reach, Analisa snatched her up and hugged her tight. Marisol returned the hug, feeling the warmth of reconnection.

"I'm so glad you're home! You're so skinny—I'm afraid I'll break you!" Analisa pushed her away to regard her at arms' length. "Your hair, just as long as it was in school and no gray! I'm so jealous. Please tell me you dye."

A little overwhelmed, Marisol laughed weakly. "I don't. Sorry."

Analisa looked down at her own plump form with a self-conscious grin. "I know. I've changed. But such is life when you're a *solterona*, hmm? An old maid?"

"I… I guess."

Marisol didn't understand what made her so

tongue-tied. Maybe spending so much time on the Internet talking with people through her fingers hampered her ability to conduct face-to-face communication. If so, this weekend would prove good for her.

The other woman hesitated, studying her a minute, and slipped an arm around Marisol's shoulders. "Come on! I've got iced tea, just the way my *abuela* used to make it, remember, with cinnamon and orange? Leave all that stuff. We'll get it later."

Marisol barely grabbed her huge purse as Analisa half-dragged her along with excitement.

"How was your flight? I don't believe you didn't bring the little man to town with you! Evil woman that you are."

"He'll be better off with my father. In case we're tempted to do something embarrassing."

"Oh, girl! I can think of a hundred things."

Analisa took her into the cheery kitchen with its yellow gingham curtains and tablecloth. She let go, finally, to fill two tall glasses on the counter with tea from a crystal pitcher.

Marisol glanced around. The appliances were all upscale, all with extras she longed for but couldn't afford just yet. Everything in Analisa's kitchen matched. The realization provoked a little sigh of envy.

"So tell me what you've been up to down in Florida. Sun and fun, right? It must be true, with that bikini body." Analisa shared her own envious sigh, and Marisol felt somewhat better.

"Just work. And Mark. That takes all my time."

She sipped the tea, the bite of spice and sweet tang of citrus refreshing her, if not sparking her tongue to chat. Analisa, always the talkative one, hardly let Marisol get a word in, and that worked just fine. Her forte was the written word; even back home, she remained shy and soft-spoken.

What I need is a little Jerrika Jones in these face to face conversations.

The thought reminded her of her resolve to reveal herself this weekend as the popular blogger. Analisa was asking her where she worked. *Time to try out the truth.*

The words tripped over her lips, though, when she attempted to speak. "I… Well, you know, bloggers. I mean… Do you use the Internet?" She flushed red. "Stupid question. Of course you use the Internet. Who doesn't?"

Analisa stared at her blankly.

"*Mira*, I'll show you."

Marisol pulled her laptop out of her bag and set it on the table. "Do you have wireless?"

Analisa cracked up. "Wait, wait, wait. Little Marisol Herrera, who sewed her own finger on the machine in Mrs. Martin's home ec' class? The girl who couldn't figure out which end of a plug to put in the wall? You're a computer whiz?"

Marisol rolled her eyes. "Please, *querida*. Just hook me up, and I'll show you."

A few minutes later, she pulled up Jerrika's bold page. *Mothering Without a Man* splashed in strong white letters across a dark red banner at the top of the screen. In the corner above the sidebar, posed the cartoonish drawing of Jerrika—a tall, thin, sharply-dressed woman with features reflecting Marisol's own ethnic heritage. A friend of hers created the toon, drawing the image chic and sassy. Definitely all Jerrika Jones.

She turned the small computer screen to Analisa.

Her friend's eyes narrowed as she scanned the page. "Oh, yeah. I've heard about her. She was on the radio with Katy Blaine last summer. We were all listening on the floor in the nurses' lounge. She was funny as heck, that Jerrika. Giving men in general what-for, ragging on deadbeat dads. She…"

Analisa trailed off as Marisol looked her steadily in the eye.

"She… *Dios mio*, Mari. Are you telling me you're…her?"

Marisol grinned at her friend's trembling finger, pointed at the screen, and confessed, "I'm her."

Analisa's gasp seemed to go on until Marisol wondered if she would ever breathe again.

"That's where you *work*? You make money? Do they really pay you to write the column, Mari? Are you going to be rich and famous?"

Gratified at the hint of envy in her friend's eyes, Marisol laughed. "I don't know about rich and famous, Ana, but so far the ads pay the bills. That's all I need, for now." She winked. "After Mark goes off to school? Who knows?"

Analisa babbled on. "Wow. I thought Sammy Lynn was the only one from our class who ever, you know, got famous."

"I saw her once in Cincinnati, singing at a live concert. Not too long after we graduated. I loved her music. She really had soul." Marisol sighed, thinking how the music touched her. "Then she just disappeared. Does anyone know if she's coming back for the reunion?"

"I haven't seen her. But then I've been working lots of hours. Since we're the only full-service hospital in the area, we get hit every weekend with any kind of trauma you can imagine. On the floors, we aren't as bad off as they are downstairs, of course, but we still stay busy. Tourist season is the *worst.* Some weekends I think I hardly see the sun."

She gestured to her full-figured body. "Hence the shape I'm in."

She shrugged and finished her tea. "Lakeside Medical Center applied for a grant from the Whitmore Foundation to fund a wellness program for the medical professionals. Kind of ironic, hmm? But if that comes through, they'll give us time on shift to work out."

Marisol tapped on the arrowed button to scroll down to the comments on her last post, curious as always to see what people thought of her columns. A growl rose in her throat as she recognized a frequent commenter to her blog, FreeDad91.

It's all very well for you to say that children don't need a mother and *a father, but frankly, Jerrika, how do you know? Just because you, in your infinite wisdom, have shut your child's father out of his life, how do you know that he wouldn't have turned out differently, so much better and balanced, if he'd had the chance to share his father's life, too?*

"What's the matter, *chica*?"

Analisa leaned close to read over her shoulder. Her friend's little intake of breath demonstrated a similar hostile reaction to the comment.

"But you didn't throw Mark's father out of his

life." Analisa poured them both more tea, a large helping of indignant thick in her voice.

"No. Kirby walked out on us all on his own."

Mark had just turned three when Kirby Slade decided marriage and fatherhood didn't suit him. At least he'd left a note saying he was gone for good, and she didn't have to worry about him coming back. She could have used some of his money over the years, but she used her mother's lessons well, scraping what little money she made waitressing as thin as she could to make sure Mark had food and clothes and school.

I always knew I'd come in as a priority later. After he was grown.

It was almost time.

"These trolls don't care about the truth, Ana. They're just trying to score points for their own ego."

FreeDad91's jab hurt more than she wanted to admit, certainly more than Jerrika ever would. She tried to hold her alter ego's shield of boldness up to protect herself. She hadn't attacked him directly. It didn't seem fair that he'd do it to her. So what if this guy didn't agree with her? The Internet was certainly big enough for two people to have differing opinions. But he didn't have to be rude.

She could delete the comment under the standard rules of her blog, well-identified in the sidebar, since he'd used the profanity. But she decided not to. She knew others would share his views, and still others would oppose them, and that would draw more people into the discussion and increase the number of posts to the blog.

More posters meant more numbers, and more numbers proved her as a good investment to potential advertisers. Fifteen thousand-plus readers in the last year convinced the baby food people to purchase a spot on the blog. More would be better.

Marisol frowned and read the paragraph again. FreeDad91, whoever he was, certainly wrote from an angry place, a place of pain. She wondered idly whether he'd caused his own portion of hell on earth, or whether it dropped on him, like hers did. She'd tracked back to his own blog, entitled "Why does Life Hate Me?" in an effort to see if she could glean details. Most of the posts ended up in woman-hating rants, but she recognized a thread of need and longing in them as well. She didn't recognize the name—Stuart something—so his attacks weren't really personal, not in the way of someone who actually knew her. What was this dad missing?

Analisa's smile widened. "Are you going to blast him now? Can I watch? I'll tell everyone I was there when Mr. Thing got his comeuppance."

A faint smile crossed Marisol's lips and faded as she closed her browser and turned off the machine. She'd learned early in her blogging career that a sharp, angry response posted quickly, but became much harder to retract. Better to think about it and post something once she'd armored up.

"Not now. I'll wait until I come up with something really spectacular."

"You'd better do it while you're here. I don't want to miss a word!"

Marisol promised she would and changed the subject, wanting the afternoon to head in a more positive direction. She'd come all this way to have fun, and she certainly intended to follow through with it.

"So, Ana, tell me all about what we're going to do

this weekend."

Chapter Four

Russell Asher cruised into West Exeter the Wednesday night before the reunion weekend in his aging silver Lexus, focused on feeling on top of his world.

He'd stay with his parents for the weekend, not in the big old three-bedroom house he and his brothers grew up in on Mount Hope Road, but in the elders' new condo on the lake. Their living space in the condo community, smaller and easier for them to manage, also provided them with luxuries such as a pool and fitness room their middle-class home didn't include. He intended to take advantage of every luxury he couldn't afford in his own place.

When Joshua and Kate Asher decided to downsize the year before, Russell had overseen the process, as the only son living nearby. His two brothers had both turned their college degrees into firm government careers and had moved south to the D.C. area. Kate never hesitated to ask Russell to help out; that's why he was home at least every other month.

He'd checked with Kate by phone when he stopped to fill up, making sure she'd wait dinner for him since he got out of the office so late. He smiled when she said she'd chucked a package of ribs in the crock pot that morning just for him. His mama, an old Tennessee gal, made some smokin' ribs. His stomach rumbled just thinking about the spicy, tomato-thick aroma that would come off them when she opened the lid at the table. He stepped a little harder on the gas.

Deep Purple's "Smoke on the Water" came on the classic rock station he'd been listening to while driving, and he cranked up the volume till the bass shook the car. He pounded his thumb on the side of the steering wheel in rhythm as he pulled into a visitors' spot at the condo village, trying to forget how many of his high-school-era songs the DJ had designated as "classic" this trip.

He was *not* old. No way.

Grabbing the worn gray suitcases he'd used since college, he locked the car doors and found his parents' building, taking the stairs two at a time, just to prove to himself he still could. His mother opened the door even before he knocked. She must have seen him out the lace-curtained window. The house smelled like barbecue heaven.

"Mama." He hugged her and kissed her cheek. "You look beautiful."

"Ha!" she replied tartly. "You didn't even look. You just want my barbecue."

Knowing she was right, he grinned. She'd lost a little more weight, exactly what the doctor wanted, and she seemed to stand a little taller. Her back must not pain her so much. She'd lost nothing in the amused sparkle of her dark eyes, though. "Sorry, Mama."

She hugged him all the same. "Go wash up. Your daddy's nearly gnawed off the arm of his chair the last half hour."

"Yes, ma'am."

He dropped his luggage in the guest room, then

ducked into the half bath near the door. This was his father's customary retreat to sit and read, and reflected that use: very basic, toilet, sink, wastebasket, tall basket for news magazines and the local paper, a couple of towels. No folderol or decorations everywhere, just the necessities. And a locking door to prevent being disturbed. *Perfect.*

When he returned, his father, his hair a little more gray and the circles under his eyes a little deeper than the last time Russell had seen him, sat at the head of the table. The dining room was small, and the table smaller; it seated only four, not the eight that the table had in their old house. But the cloth was clean, white and embroidered with small daisies, that he was sure his mother had done by hand. Pictures of the family at various points in their lives graced the wall behind the table, a reminder that they all traveled together, whether at their childhood home, or this new one.

Russell came around the end of the table to embrace his old man and took the seat at his right.

"How are you, Dad?" he asked. A closer look told him that his father's skin held a hint of tan. He must have been spending time outdoors, perhaps golfing. That was a good thing.

"Oh, not so bad. Retirement agrees with me, so far. Haven't driven your mother crazy yet."

"That's what *you* think," Kate said as she carried in the creamy potato salad. Her traditional barbecue side dish always came packed with fresh peas and just a bit of green onion for bite. And always Hellmann's Mayonnaise. Rusty had made the mistake of bringing home a jar of Miracle Whip from the store once. That was all it took.

"Hush, woman." Joshua grinned with fondness for his bride of forty-some years. "Feed me."

Russell observed them with a pang of longing. This was what adult life was supposed to be—a long-term relationship of mutual respect, a couple working to raise their children together, to make a good life for the family. Not his bachelor apartment in a high-rise where he still lived out of boxes after eight months.

"This food is delicious, Mama," he said, wolfing down his first helping before reaching for his second. It beat the hell out of frozen TV dinners and fast food.

"Honestly, Rusty, you'd think you were a high school boy in a growing spurt, the way you're going at that." She smiled and passed him the potato salad.

"You and the old team getting together?" his father asked.

"Yes, sir. We're supposed to meet down at Napoli's later."

"Just like the old days. At least you don't have to borrow the car."

His dad's brown eyes twinkled, and Russell grinned back, still focused on the good time he would soon enjoy. "Yes, sir."

Kate ate her dinner without much comment. When they finished, Russell started to excuse himself, but his mother cleared her throat. He read what she wanted to say in her eyes and sighed.

"Rusty, while you're home, I wanted you to talk to Tiffany. About the boys."

"Mama, you know I've tried—"

"We went to their baseball game last week. Jon cut us dead." Tears came into her eyes. "Sweet Jesus, Rusty, we're their grandparents. All we want is to be a part of their lives, even if we don't have as much money as the high and mighty Kearnses. We're still good people."

He choked back the hurt that rose like bile in his throat at the sound of his mother's pain. "I know, Mama. It's not like I see them any more than that. She's determined…" He trailed off. No sense in adding his own pain to his mother's. Lord knows, she'd carry both of them.

Damn Tiffy.

Even if she wanted to hurt him for the circumstances of his birth, his parents didn't deserve to be punished. They loved Jon and Barret dearly. He'd seen the scrapbooks Kate crafted with clippings from the paper and photographs of the boys' accomplishments since they were small. The Kearns family members, of course, always made the paper.

Even when their last names were Asher.

At least Tiffy hadn't been able to take that away, not yet.

His voice barely able to push past his constricted throat, he got up. "Sure, Mama. I'll talk to her."

He stacked several of the empty dishes on his own plate and carried them into the kitchen, setting them on the marbled Formica counter near the sink. Before his mother could catch up with him, he escaped into the main bath and locked the door. A hot shower would do him good, wash all that guilt away, wouldn't it?

The handles cranked easily. Soon the bathroom filled with clouds of steam, with no window to release it.

But even as the stinging beads of water beat on his stressed body, he couldn't stop thinking about the situation with Tiffy. About his part in it.

He could have forced visitation, for himself and for his parents, if he made the effort through the court. Surely Gordon Kearns didn't control every judge in the state. But Russell had never taken that step. He'd always backed away, unable to stand the look that came over his former wife and his two sons, almost in unison when they saw him. That identical look of disgust. Of total acknowledgment he was worth nothing in their eyes, and never would be.

He couldn't stand it.

He stood under the spray and let it hit his face.

His focus was definitely fraying.

When he was thoroughly soaked, he shut off the water and stepped out onto the peach-colored bathmat made in the shape of a scallop shell. His mother loved the ocean, or at least the idea of it. He didn't remember a single vacation they'd taken there, yet here it was. Jars of shells decorated the counter around the sink, and several cheap pictures of beach scenes hung on the walls.

Belatedly, he realized he'd come into the bathroom without a change of clothes. Wrapping the towel around him, he inched out the door and ran to the guest bedroom. He set his suitcase on one of the twin beds, digging for the clothes he wanted to wear. The empty beds, with matching coverlets had been purchased with the intention of a future visit from the boys, even though they'd certainly never come. Ever hopeful, that described Kate. She held faith in people.

He couldn't say the same about himself. Not anymore.

****

Shooting pool at Napoli's seemed to him more like the glory days, especially since the pub's owner, Jake "The Snake" Torrelli, graduated from Wright High, too, although a couple of years before Russell. He decorated the place with all sorts of West Exeter memorabilia: trophies, pennants, photos, even one of Russell's senior basketball team at the state tournament where they came in third place.

It was a minor point of honor, but his fifteen minutes of fame was still important. He counted to someone, somewhere.

In honor of the reunion, Jake loaded the jukebox with eighties music, so the tunes just kept coming, and not the crappy girly stuff like Foreigner, either. Strictly "big hair" rock and roll bands, Quiet Riot, Poison, and Queensrÿche, which played now "Eyes of a Stranger."

In that beat, he could definitely lose himself.

A lot of people patronized Napoli's for a Thursday. They jammed nearly shoulder to shoulder at the bar, although the crowd thinned out in the open. A couple of older women swayed to the music as they peered through the glass at the tiny words on the juke's list. He thought they looked familiar, but not enough so to venture a wrong guess as to their identity.

As he waited for his turn to shoot, a pudgy bald man shoved his way through to the cash register, elbowing Russell as he passed. Russell wavered left to right, succeeding in not spilling his beer, and growled at the man, who turned to give him the eye.

Instead, he stopped and stared.

"Russell Asher? Holy smokes, you haven't hardly changed at all!" The man looked Russell up and down. He greeted Russell's companions, James Thompson and Stuart Fry, adding, "Don't you recognize me?"

Russell had to confess he didn't. He debated suggesting the man was the high school janitor, but held his tongue.

"It's me, Marty Drogan! From the basketball team. Man, are you blind?"

Astounded one of his teammates could look like a sixty-year-old guy, Russell set down his beer and offered his hand. "It's been a long time, man. How you doing?" he asked, though he wasn't really sure he wanted to know.

"Can't complain, can't complain." Drogan reached into his worn suit pocket and slapped a business card into Russell's outstretched hand. "Been in sales fifteen years. Working my way up to V.P. any day now." A big cheesy grin. "Me and Carrie have a big house out on Lake Drive."

"'Not my Cherry Carrie? How's she doing?"

James shook his head violently behind Drogan's shoulder and made a face.

"Carrie's the sweetest little thing ever, that good little woman who makes my day," Drogan said. "She just sent me to pick up some pizza. We'll see you at the reunion, right?"

"Ah… sure. Sure you will."

Drogan bustled off, all puffed up with pride. Russell turned to James. "What was that about?"

"Man, that Carrie put on about a ton with those kids of hers. No one in that house is starving, if you get my drift."

"Too bad. She was pretty cute back in the day."

"Coulda hit that."

"As if."

"Maybe I could."

Russell let his thoughts wander along memory lane to the old days, when he, Marty, James, and the others scored baskets on the gym floor, then scored more private points after the game with the cheerleaders. James had dated Cherise Lang for a short time. Marty and Carrie hooked up early. Tiffy came around a little later.

Maybe he should have taken that as a hint. An omen. Leave the girl alone and find someone less ostentatious and more solid... Other girls showed interest in him. He'd been pretty steady with Marisol Herrera for the summer after junior year, till the basketball season started in the fall of senior year. She was sweet, and she always helped him with his English essays. Writing had never been one of his strong points. But when Tiffy came around, he'd just blown her off for a shot at the stars.

"Russ, man, your shot. Wake up!" Stuart poked him in the kidney with his cue stick.

"Ow! Yeah, yeah, I'm going."

He surveyed the table. "Fifteen in the corner pocket."

Picturing Tiffy's face on the white ball, exactly where he aimed, he derived some real satisfaction from the firm crack his stick made against it, as well as the accurate shot setting him up to go after the eight ball. He sent that one into the depths of the pocket as well, just a passing thought about black and white disappearing into his beer as he drained the glass.

"Who's buying the next round?" he asked.

"You won, hot shot. Must be you!"

James and Stu broke into raucous laughter, and

Russell grinned. Yes, back with his buds, the right music playing, and if he had enough beer, he'd be able to put Tiffy right out of his mind. Or at least hide her so thoroughly he could avoid thinking about her for one night.

He hoped that was enough.

Chapter Five

On Friday, Analisa went to her seven a.m. shift at the hospital, leaving Marisol a pan of fresh-baked Pillsbury cinnamon rolls and strong coffee. They'd made plans for dinner later with some of the girls from the old neighborhood.

None of them, of course, was rich enough or important enough to attend the biggest event in West Exeter that weekend, the black-tie dinner sponsored by the Whitmore Foundation. So, for her social group, it was just another working day. Marisol was on her own.

Finding her way around the unfamiliar kitchen became an adventure into wishing territory, as she confirmed just how many fancy gadgets Ana owned. But before long, Marisol found some beautifully painted plates and a coffee mug bearing a Niagara Falls logo, and she settled in for breakfast.

Anxiety and guilt set in at her just sitting. At home, she'd worry about the dishes drying on the counter, or the load of Mark's jeans waiting by the washing machine. No way could she sit at the table while all those chores awaited. Not that she was OCD or anything, but, over the years, she'd just come to believe life worked more smoothly when she took care of issues as soon as they came up. Be proactive, not reactive. This made her feel more in control. Less like she had to depend on someone else.

But here, in Ana's kitchen, no agenda and no chores awaited her. She really could just sit and drink her coffee in peace.

Which, of course, after two sips, meant she absolutely couldn't, without going mad.

Stuffing a bite of gooey cinnamon roll in her mouth, she ran back to the guest room for her laptop. She brought it back to the table and, while the browser loaded, she did Ana a favor and put away last night's dinner dishes, stacked on a wooden rack under the open window.

Outside, children called to one another in Spanglish, as they had when Ana and Mari were that age. Most of the parents spoke Spanish inside the home, but the kids adapted to the life and culture of America much more easily. Their children, like Mark, hardly used Spanish at all, but he spoke it fluently. Marisol had found the ability to speak two languages very useful over the years, especially in the jobs she'd held before graduating to full-time blogging status.

Refilling her cup, she curled into the padded rattan chair at the table and signed into Jerrika's Facebook page. Thirty-five more people had requested Jerrika Jones as their friend over the last week, bringing her total to nearly five thousand. Hundreds more Liked her fan page, and the conversation there proved spirited and intimate. Single moms had a lot to say nearly every day.

Marisol had her personal page, too. Marisol had maybe a dozen friends. Not quite the same at all.

Several more people had commented on her blog post from the day before. Others filed comments slamming FreeDad91, especially some of her six hundred regular readers, whose names she recognized from her subscription list. Some of them had been with her since she'd first started out.

Everyone was entitled to an opinion, wasn't that true?

She considered what to say, pulling apart the cinnamon roll on her painted plate. Analisa's dishware pattern swirled in beautiful florals. Imagine owning a cabinet full of matching dishes! Again the Green-Eyed monster stung her. If she was lucky, she could find two the same for herself and Mark some nights.

"That's why you can survive on what the writing pays, *chica*," she scolded herself aloud. "Because you aren't attached to material things."

All the same, a better class of things would be nice, wouldn't they?

She needed to boost her readership another five thousand to get more ads. Other options hovered on the horizon, too. Heather Armstrong had books out now, spawned by the popularity of her Dooce blog. The *Julie and Julia* movie deal started with a simple blog. That Shatner show on TV, "*$#*! My Dad Says*" came from a Twitter account. If she could get noticed, really noticed, the big time wasn't so far away in this brave new Internet world.

So. Better to stir the pot, right?

She closed her eyes, summoned up the image of Jerrika at her cheekiest, and started typing.

Apparently I stomped on a couple of hearts yesterday when I pointed out the joys of raising my son without having to kowtow to the demands of an irrational non-custodial father. You know what? I'm not sorry, either.

People like FreeDad91 hide in their troll costumes

and take pot shots at other people instead of addressing their own issues.

Sounds to me like this guy has problems from his past. Either his own father walked out on him, or he walked out on his own kids, and he's decided the best way to handle his guilt is to dump on the mothers.

Well, honey, this is one mother who's not going to just sit by and let you. I love my son dearly. He's been my morning, my evening, and lots of my midnights over the years. Maybe he didn't have a father by his side during those days and nights. But he never lacked for attention, from men or women. I made sure he had that village he needed, the one it takes to raise a child. Would it have been easier to co-parent? I expect it would have. But that option wasn't open to me. So take your hatred and turn it back where it really belongs: on yourself.

She added a few more choice stabs, and filed the post for the day.

By the time she checked in again that evening, she'd certainly find a whole host of angry responses. But that was all right. Jerrika could handle that, with her thick skin. Marisol would be out with her friends, relaxing.

She closed her laptop and disconnected it before heading to the shower, amused by the split-personality thinking process she used to rationalize her reactions. The dichotomy wasn't pathological; she was always Marisol Slade. But sometimes, that strong costume of the tall dark-skinned woman helped her stand up for her beliefs. Mari had made Jerrika famous. It was the least she could do in return.

****

Just before noon, Marisol drove into town to find something to eat and renew some memories. She pulled her car in along the south side of the street at the Diamond, a grassy park in the center of town, dotted with war memorials and other local commemorations. She walked out into the middle of the landscaped area, looked up at the tall trees, remembering events here— holiday speeches, and one special performance when she sang in the school choir—all delivered from the gazebo stage. Her mother sat on the bench to the left, her face aglow while her daughter sang. How old had Marisol been? Maybe eleven, twelve? She climbed the two steps to the stage and tried to recapture the feeling of pride she'd experienced when her mother watched her performance. What had the choir sung? Some rock song her *abuela* thought too adult for a children's chorus, that much she remembered. She'd complained all night after they went home. "We Are Family," maybe. The spring air had held just the slightest chill and, with her mother's permission, she'd worn her new white sweater—the one suitable only for church so far. With smoothly brushed hair, and barrettes matching her dress fastened in just the right places, and she believed she was beautiful. Her mother's smile proved it true.

Until Tiffany Kearns' solo. She had shoved her way into place in the front row next to Marisol. The spoiled brat hardly noticed her, planting an elbow right in Marisol's budding chest. It hurt so much, tears filled her eyes, but she couldn't show it, not with Mama smiling there in the audience. She forced herself to act strong.

I was always competing with that girl, even from the very beginning. The funny thing is, she never even knew it.

A bird singing overhead returned Marisol's attention to the present, but the blonde woman getting out of the car parked in front of Marisol's could be no other than the just-remembered Tiffany Kearns.

Of course, the license plate "KEARNS3" served as a dead giveaway.

But wasn't her name Asher?

Two boys followed her from the baby blue Chevy Tahoe SUV, dressed in nearly-identical knee-length chinos and casually pastel polo shirts, the kind that ran to nearly a hundred dollars at upscale mall stores. They slouched after their mother to a shop farther up the block. They sported blond hair, but she saw their skin, their dark eyes, so much like Russell's at that age. No doubt these were Russell's boys.

He didn't get out of the car with them, though.

So where was he?

Would he be here this weekend?

Maybe she'd pushed him out of her mind in preparation for being here—focusing on the parts that she knew would be fun and light-hearted. Time to use that Jerrika armor again.

She came down off the gazebo, feeling a little exposed. It didn't seem to her that anyone was watching her, not her specifically. Members of the community went about their business of a Friday morning, surely the same sorts of things that people did in every small city across the country.

Somehow Marisol had never seen it that way when she'd been in school. Her father had supervised a work crew for a local farmer, her mother worked in the hardware store, and she and her two brothers and two sisters worked, too, as soon as they were old enough, to supplement the family income. Sometimes they got to keep a little of their own for spending money. Not very often.

She'd wanted to make life different for Mark. At home in Ocala, Marisol tried to make sure she was the one who kept the bills paid. She managed well enough. Her rent got paid by running an answering service for her landlord weekends and evenings from her own living room, and the sponsors and donations from the blog helped keep the day-to-day expenses under control.

Fortunately, she and Mark had always been healthy, and she had the SunTran public transportation system memorized. She got by without a car for the most part, which saved her a lot. Mark could take her places she needed to go sometimes, in the car he'd paid for, if she couldn't get there otherwise. It all worked.

She started for the Sweet Spot coffee shop across the street, but hesitated when a silver Lexus squealed a U-turn in the center of Main, screeching to a stop and blocking her little rental there in its parking place. The door flew open, practically ejecting a tall, well-built man in jeans and a blue cotton shirt. His full attention focused on the vehicle in front of Marisol's.

She couldn't move as she belatedly recognized his large dark eyes and something in the piqued set of his jaw.

Russell Asher.

His hair wasn't as solidly black as she'd remembered from the summer she left town. The jeans, no longer slim cut, though he wasn't overweight. But it was him.

Nausea tumbled like panicked butterflies in her stomach. One hand slipped to her middle, almost trying to reassure her insides not to make her throw up right here. She never expected a sudden confrontation. She hadn't prepared.

But as she watched him, she saw she didn't need to worry. He wasn't interested in her in the least. He marched over to the SUV and parked himself against its shiny fender. After several tries, she forced her feet to move, at least far enough to retreat inside the gazebo. She sat on the interior edge of the fence, half hidden behind a painted support beam, the shade from the maples overhead helping to conceal her. She couldn't help it. She could have walked away, just left her vehicle and come back for it later, but the situation was a car wreck waiting to happen. She could tell by the tension in his shoulders and his hands, clenched into fists. No way she would miss whatever occurred next.

Soon after, Tiffany and the boys, one of whom looked about Mark's age, one a little younger, returned from the shop. Tiffany, thin to the point of anorexia, stopped several yards from her car when she saw Russell there. The boys hung back behind their mother, affecting bored poses of crossed arms and blank skyward stares.

"What do you want, Rusty?" Her voice carried clearly to the gazebo.

"To say hello to Jon and Barret. Since you haven't let them come see me for the last three months." He didn't move off the car. "Hey, boys, come give your old dad a hug, hmm?"

The boys mumbled something Marisol couldn't hear. If anything, they retreated toward the store, and finally the younger of the two, who looked maybe fifteen, bolted, heading back inside.

"That's fabulous, Tiffy, just fabulous. What a great mother you are. So much for what our order says, right? That we're supposed to encourage the children to love and honor the other parent?"

"What have you done worth honoring? Hmm?"

Tiffany's voice still cut like a knife. Marisol had been the recipient of that sarcasm herself on more than one occasion. The pitch had aged well over the years, like a fine wine.

"They're my sons. They're my parents' grandchildren. You can't keep them from us."

Marisol watched his face, peeking from around the post. His shoulders hunched over, and he didn't face Tiffany directly, but turned to the side just a little. Four years of therapy after Kirby Slade left her taught her about body language and presenting herself strong.

Russell Asher radiated…fear.

Movement behind Tiffany drew Marisol's eye. A tall, well-dressed white man came out of the store with the younger boy, an arm around his shoulders, and the two walked over to stand with Tiffany.

"Is there a problem here?" the man said.

Russell pushed himself upright and squared himself to the newcomer. *Now he gets a backbone. Must be a guy thing. What was he going to do?*

"None of your business, Paul. Go on back to your cravats and high-end socks, will you?"

"Tiffany and the boys *are* my business now," the man said. "The sooner you learn that, the better everyone's life will be."

He stepped in front of Tiffany in a gesture as clear

as rolling up his sleeves.

Russell eyed him for several long moments, during which Marisol wondered if he'd actually have a fist-fight on the street. *Here comes the car wreck.* She held her breath.

Finally he shoved his hands in his pocket and laughed. "Don't worry, Pauly. You won't have to get your hands dirty. I'll handle this my way." He choked over his next words. "Bye, Jon. Barret. I'll see you for dinner Sunday."

He started to walk away, across Main Street.

"Got plans, Dad. Maybe next time."

That was the older one. He stood at his mother's elbow, a defiant smirk on his lips.

Russell stopped and straightened his shoulders, though he didn't turn back around. "Pick you up at four."

He continued to his car, got in, and gunned the engine.

The four on the sidewalk conferred hurriedly, then mother and sons retreated to her car. Paul returned wherever he'd come from. Marisol could breathe again. Something had happened to Russell and Tiffany. She could hardly wait till dinner that night to find out what.

Chapter Six

Russell burned all the way back to his parents'
house. One single piece of good fortune salvaged the
moment—his father's doctor's appointment kept his
parents away from home for the afternoon.

He slammed the car door, furious that Tiffy
continued her flawed alienation of the boys. She
couldn't even deal with him herself; she had to involve
that pretty boy from the clothing store. Paul Dupont
probably earned Gordon's approval; his ancestry likely
dated back to the Pilgrims.

Well, to be honest, he scolded himself, his boy
involved the twerp, not Tiffy.

But she let him.

Inside, he grabbed a Killian's Red from the
refrigerator, grateful he'd persuaded his old man to
switch from the generic stuff he drank when Russell
was a boy. That stuff tasted like water. He downed half
of it before he got back to the bedroom. He needed to
blow something up. Seriously.

He activated his laptop and sat back, guzzling the
beer while he waited. As soon as the browser launched,
he punched in the Web site for his game. A mission or
two destroying enemy bases would release some of the
anger seething through him.

Before the game loaded, though, the cackle of a
parrot went off, informing him of a Facetime request.

He clicked through to the request on his phone, knowing the graphics-heavy game would take longer to load. It was from Stuart.

"Asher, have you seen this crap? I mean, have you seen it?"

The angry outburst was followed by screenshot after screenshot of Jerrika Jones' latest blog.

Russell was in the mood for anything else but hearing about how great single mothers were. What had the woman said now?

The words flowed across the screen, and a justified resentment bubbled up in him. Maybe she was right for her particular situation, but when he filtered his own situation through her words, he knew she didn't understand what life was like for the fathers. Not at all.

"Women. Castrating witches, that's what they are!" Stuart was off the rails. "You can't tell me that wasn't directed right at me. How dare she? How *dare* she? If I could get my hands on her…"

"Come on, Stuart, get a grip. Okay, she's making it personal. I don't know why. But you flying off the handle isn't going to solve a damn thing. She's just a cartoon and some words on your computer screen. She's probably not real. Some society gal who's building up readership by lighting things on fire. She wanted a hot reaction—don't give it to her, or she wins."

"Someone needs to take her down a peg. Or ten."

"Right. Look, Stu. I've got problems of my own, huh?"

"Oh? Tiffany's giving you crap now? You're not going to take it, are you?"

"Hell, no, I'm not."

"That's my man! That's my man. All right, I've got to go. This chick really burns me. I'm gonna…" He closed the connection, and Russell was alone with his thoughts again.

He understood Stuart's fury. But he wasn't like that.

The man voted most likely to… What had it been? Most likely to be First Man, husband of the first woman president of the United States. Not that anyone thought Tiffany Kearns possessed enough smarts to be president, but just because they considered him the kind of man any woman would want for a husband. Especially someone famous.

But Stu really had to get a grip, and not on some woman's neck.

Russell's anger at Tiffany receded in the light of space and distance. He closed his eyes, took a few deep breaths to clear his mind, sharpen his focus, like his old coach had always taught. As his rib cage expanded and contracted, he concentrated on the movement of the air, letting go of his hostility. It didn't leave him, but it diminished.

He could deal with Tiffany in court, if it came to that. Sure, her family could bankroll a Superlawyer from out of town, but the law was the law. He was the boys' father, and he had rights. From the looks of the situation today, he probably ought to consider that alternative strongly, before he lost them altogether. Boys needed their own father. Not that starched-shirt Paul.

Jerrika Jones, on the other hand, presented a whole different issue. No need for him to impale himself on her words. He didn't know her, she meant nothing to him, and he could just tune her out with a click.

When he went back to his laptop, the browser flickered to life with the opening screen of his game, his logon blinking. His long fingers lay across the mouse, but he didn't tap in. He'd passed the need for destruction. He really just needed some social time, face time with old friends.

He turned off the computer and made his way to the kitchen where he threw together a pair of sandwiches from some wheat buns and his mother's leftover barbecue to soak up the brew. He ate the sandwich hurriedly and headed out to see where he might find the rest of his former classmates.

****

Avoiding Diamond Park and its recent memories, Russell cruised downtown and finally chose a parking place on State Street. Opening his email app, he checked the list the reunion committee sent for possible venues of reunion weekend events.

What didn't make the list, but he'd read about in a newspaper article that morning, was the Talon award dinner. Even as a successful, white-collar graduate, he hadn't received an invitation for that, probably because Tiffany used her pull with the Powers That Be. She wouldn't want him ruining her twisted perception of her self-image, after all.

He spotted the one class gathering planned for mid-afternoon, an activity he bet would repeat late tonight. The pancake place out on the arterial opened its back room for the afternoon to Wright grads, one and all. Those who brought a reunion invitation would get free coffee, no doubt in honor of all those nights most of them had been there till three a.m. drinking cup after cup and sharing a large order of fries because it was the one place open after midnight.

Might be worth checking out, just for the random drop-bys.

Fifteen minutes later, he popped his collar, like they did in the old days, and strolled on in. He didn't recognize any of the eager young waitstaff, of course, though he didn't hold back from checking out their legs under their short skirts. They smiled as they showed him back to the meeting room and ruined everything by calling him, "sir."

"Rusty!"

He heard his name called by at least three women. He scanned the wood-paneled room and spotted them seated at a head table with dark green print fabric on the booth seats. They waved and smiled at him like good hostesses. A CD player on a side table played a series of hit songs popular the year they graduated. Distracted by the assortment of fake antiques nailed out of reach along the wall, he did his best to guess the women's identities.

Angela... He recognized the blonde but couldn't remember her married name. She used to do the morning announcements. *Suck-up.* Next to her sat Debbie Emanuel, one of those perky girls who made friends with anyone and everyone—and looked like she still did. She maintained the kind of body a woman got from constant activity, probably tennis, biking, maybe even skiing. She looked good.

He'd thought about asking her out in their earlier years, but she'd always been so involved in her activities, she never had time. The third woman, he had no idea... Someone who'd put on about a hundred pounds… O-o-h, maybe that was Carrie. He eyed her a minute and really hoped not.

"Hello, ladies," he said in his most suave manner. He needed to flirt a little, to redeem himself after the disastrous meeting with Tiffy.

Debbie stood up and put out her hand to greet him. Her hazel green eyes flashed a warm welcome. "Debbie Emanuel—now Vogan. I got married after college. So glad to see you."

"You, too," he said. "What are you up to these days?"

"Well, you remember how many plays I did in school, right? I got my theatre degree and now I'm a movie director." Her face lit up. "Nothing big, yet, mostly short films and documentaries, but I think I might be nominated for a national award this year."

"That's really great to hear."

Debbie grinned at him. "I was hoping you'd come. We're just planning some events for the dance at the gym tomorrow night, the eighties splash, you know, and I remembered you and Tiffany doing the Pee Wee Big Shoe Dance."

A flash of embarrassment ran through him as he remembered it, too. What a geek he'd been. "Oh, geeze, Debbie. Can't you remember some of what I did on the court instead?"

"We haven't forgotten that," Angela purred, her eyes hungry as she watched him. "Those thin jerseys didn't cover much."

Russell swallowed hard. "Well. I…ah…" *Maybe not that much remembering.*

"What about that Pee-Wee thing again? What was that song?"

" 'Tequila,' " came a quiet voice from behind him. He turned slowly to see who spoke.

Marisol Herrera.

Marisol Herrera Slade now. He'd seen her name in one of the interim emails from the reunion committee. So she must have gotten married after she left school. At the moment, she sat alone, though.

Marisol hadn't changed much at all: a little older through the eyes, a little tired-looking, her smile faint as if it would fade away if the light didn't stay focused on it. But she still carried herself well, her figure slim, and her sharp white tank and skirt showed it off. Older, and better, apparently.

He'd always liked her. They'd had some real good times. She was smart, kinda pretty, and always pleasant.

She just wasn't Tiffy.

"Hey, Mari." Even the familiar name sat right on his tongue as he said it. She was checking him out, too. He sucked in his stomach. *Just a little. Just in case.* "Can I join you?"

She froze for a moment, but smiled and nodded.

"Rusty!" Debbie called his attention back. "I want to make sure our schedule's complete, I's dotted and T's crossed. Can we count on you to run a "Tequila" dance contest Saturday night then?"

"Huh? Oh, sure. Sure, I can do that."

"Fabulous!" Debbie checked off some line on the clipboard in front of her. "Coffee's over there."

She pointed to a whole row of silver carafes on the sideboard designed to keep coffee warm for hours. A uniformed server waited at the end of the sideboard to take any orders to go with the free coffee. Russell shook his head and took his cup over to the table where

Marisol sat. Nice to see a friendly face after that debacle in the park. She seemed friendly, at least. If she intended to be resentful of him, considering what he'd done in the name of glory, she didn't show it. Maybe it was a case of "bygones."

When he eased into the bench seat across from her, her face flushed. She looked years younger, almost as young as when they'd been seeing each other. "You look great, Mari. You know, I don't remember seeing you around town. Are you living in the area?"

"No. I live in Florida. I haven't been back. I mean, this is the first time since… Well, since graduation, I guess." She fidgeted with the spoon on the table next to her cup, long, thin fingers rolling the utensil over and over.

Her nail polish shone some kind of medium pink, nothing as brassy as the reds Tiffy used to wear. He wanted to compliment Marisol but believed "real" men shouldn't comment on nail polish. He knew more about it than most men because of his time at Evergreen's. He'd stocked that makeup wall many times over the years, and he'd always been fascinated by the names of those enamels. They sounded exotic and delicious, with names like Raspberry Mousse, Midnight Meetings, and Barefoot in Barcelona.

But not manly. He'd save that thought.

"I've had a couple of conventions for work in the Sunshine State. What part do you live in?"

"Central Florida. Since the late nineties."

He glanced at her left hand. No ring, no tan line indicating one was missing. So Mr. Slade must be history. "By yourself?"

"No, with my son Mark." Her face lit up when she

mentioned her son. "Do you want to see a picture?" she asked, hesitant, almost as if she thought he'd refuse.

"Sure!" He drank from his cup while she dug in a small brown leather purse in her lap. His gaze floated around the room, scoping out new arrivals, but he didn't find anyone he'd rather talk to. Funny, when he'd left the house, he'd been looking for something rollicking good, something to physically shake him from his mood. But sitting quietly with Marisol calmed him even more. *There's definitely something relaxing about her.*

Marisol held out a photo, still crisp, fairly new. "This is his senior picture," she said. "He just graduated from high school."

Russell studied the picture of the dark-skinned boy with the close-cut kinky hair and the dazzling white smile, wearing a coral-colored polo shirt. He couldn't help a quick glance at Marisol, confirming he had her eyes, deep pools of emotional chocolate brown. "His father…"

She shrugged. "Gone. He ran out on us a long time ago. But Mark's come along really well. He's going to Florida State in September on a full scholarship."

"You did it yourself? Financially, I mean?"

She looked away, and he realized he'd probably crossed a personal line. Why should she explain her whole life to him in such a casual meeting? Certainly she didn't owe him anything after the way he'd treated her. *And of course, I was too young to see how crappy it was at the time. Besides being blinded by Tiffy and her family's position and power.*

He handed the picture back.

"I'm sorry, Marisol. None of my business. I was

just thinking about—"

"About Tiffany and your sons?" she asked, without looking up.

"Yeah." *How did she know that?* He silently admitted it was probably not news for most people in town. Tiffany made sure everyone knew she had disassociated herself from the half-breed. His fingers tightened involuntarily on his cup.

"We broke up ten years ago. She… Well, she divorced me." Might as well go for the sympathy vote. "I guess I always knew they'd be all right, you know, because of her dad's money," he said, feeling like he needed to explain. "I mean, we went the court route, and I always send what the courts told me to, but, ah. You know."

"Do you see them often?" she asked. Her eyes met his, vulnerable and open. He could see there the emotions just below the surface, the feelings they'd shared, feelings she was trying to hide.

"The boys?"

Did he really have to tell her the truth? What would a lie hurt?

"Sure, when they have time. At their age, they've got games and appointments and things, you know." He shrugged a little. Semi-true. Wouldn't pass a court oath. "They're very popular in town, of course, just like their mother."

She bit her bottom lip, almost as if trying to trap words inside. After a pause, she said, "I always wondered if that Kearns money and stature made you happy."

"You always…" He frowned, deciphering her meaning. "You mean, you thought about me since…

After we broke up?"

A blush filled her cheeks, but she didn't turn away.

"Why wouldn't I? I mean, after what we…" She straightened her shoulders and almost seemed to purposefully change direction. "What I mean is, not that many people in the class mattered to me, and I know I didn't matter to them." As he started to protest, she raised a hand. "No, really, I know where I stood, where my parents stood in the community. It doesn't hurt any more, not like it used to."

A twinge of guilt stabbed him. He'd really been superfocused on his goal then, mental blinders shutting out every other possibility except one. What was that Chinese proverb? Be careful what you wish for, because you may get it?

Boy, did it ever ring true now.

What would life have been like with a woman like Marisol? He'd never have scored that flat on Central Park. He might have made it through school before they had kids, might not. He studied her while she stirred her coffee again, fidgeting with her spoon. What would he have done? What might she have become?

What *had* she become?

He realized belatedly he hadn't even asked. He didn't want to look like he was prying. Maybe if he volunteered information about himself first…

"I work for Evergreen's," he said. "I just got promoted to regional liaison."

Her shy smile encouraged him. "Is that good?"

"Yes. That's good," he said, chuckling. "I've been a district manager trying to get that particular promotion for three years. Next step is regional manager. Then I could move from Cleveland back here,

I guess."

"You'd move back to where Tiffany lives? Really?"

The pure incredulity in her voice caught him up. "Well, maybe that wouldn't be the best possible scenario, huh?" He took a sip of his coffee to buy a moment to think. "I'd be closer to the boys, though. Easier to attend their sports events, and so on."

"Oh. Well, I suppose that's true."

An awkward pause passed between them, then he asked, "So what do you do?"

"I...ah...I'm a writer," she said. The spoon dropped into her cup with a clank.

That didn't surprise him. As good as she'd been in English class...isn't that what English majors did? Become writers? He stopped to consider her as an author. "Really? What do you write? Novels? Books?"

"No. Shorter...things. Articles. Columns. You know."

"Good for you," he said. "You're a successful writer, your son's about to go to college, and you look great. Good for you."

"Thanks." Her smile widened, though something in her eyes still tried to hide from his praise.

"Does your family still live here?"

After he said it, he realized it might make him look foolish. After all, he was in town fairly often, and it wasn't that big a place. *And I've just admitted I didn't care enough about them to even recognize them once in awhile.*

"No." She shrugged. "My father moved just out of town. My mother passed several years ago. All the brothers moved on. Like me." A faint smile. "Are yours?"

"They are. They're doing pretty well. They got one of those senior living condos out on the far side of the lake."

"That's great."

One of the servers came by with fresh coffee, and Russell and Marisol fell into a companionable silence while they doctored their cups with sugar and cream, stirring idly and watching other classmates come and go.

"I don't recognize most of these people," Marisol confessed.

Russell debated telling her how much Cherie had changed, which would be why she was unrecognizable, but thought better of it. "I know what you mean. I ran into Marty Drogan from the basketball team last night—I thought he was just another old man!"

They both laughed.

"We're definitely getting into that category," she said wistfully. "But if all I've done in the last twenty years is launch my son into a good life, it will be worth every wrinkle and gray hair ever."

He raised an eyebrow at that, as she had neither. But he could solidly feel how proud she was of her son. *What a shame a father had walked away from a boy like that.*

"Are you going to the dance tomorrow night?" he finally asked, gesturing back at Janice, who was now beckoning him from the greeter's table. "Or do famous writers go to the uptown event?"

"I hadn't really decided." She laid the spoon down and tucked her hands in her lap.

"Well, I just got suckered in. I'd love to see you

there."

As the words came out, he realized they held more truth than he'd actually intended. She'd always been pleasant, and she seemed interested in him still. Going to a dance stag wouldn't be right—especially if word got back to Tiffy. And he knew it would. Better to make it seem like his life was all sunshine and rainbows, too, right?

"Thanks. I'll see you then," she said, and she quickly scooted out of her chair and grabbed her purse. "I'm meeting Ana for dinner. So I'll...um, see you tomorrow then?" Nearly tripping over her sudden smile, she skittered out the door.

Russell felt very much the hero then, patting himself on the back for promising to show the shy country mouse a good time at the big event. He'd show her a good time. Maybe he'd even make up for overlooking her all those years ago.

He left his half-drunk coffee on the table and headed for the door, waving to a couple of other classmates who'd come in to visit with the ladies at the table. His weekend was looking up, definitely back on the right track now.

Chapter Seven

Giddy as she drove to the steakhouse to meet her old girlfriends, Marisol almost giggled. Russell Asher had come to her, asked to sit with her, and nearly asked her for a date?

She shouldn't read too much into that. He hadn't *actually* asked her. She ought to anticipate that he was just keeping his options open—just like he had in school.

But his expression appeared very sincere when he said he wanted me to come to the school dance.

If it hadn't been made clear by what she witnessed in the park, he'd said it himself: He and Tiffany weren't together anymore.

She couldn't decide if knowing that fact made her want to gloat, or feel sorry for them…or even be a little happy that she might be able to handle things like an adult and anticipate a pleasant evening with him at the dance. Seeing him again had certainly touched off all the old bells in her heart. For the first time, she hadn't experienced only pain when the thought of him came to her. Even if only for one night, she wondered if spending this evening in his company would heal some very old wounds, the ones that drove her away from this community to begin with. It could be a very good thing.

For a moment she almost wished she'd brought

Mark along, so he could see her be happy while attending this event, even if nothing worked out. But he was better off with his grandfather. Or should be anyway.

She hoped the two hadn't driven each other crazy yet. Maybe she should check on him.

When she pulled into the half-filled parking lot of the steakhouse, she turned off the car, wondering if she had parked in direct proximity to the exhaust fans from inside. The aroma of grilled meats and garlic bread floated in the air all around her. Her stomach growling, she realized lunch happened far too long ago, and multiple cups of coffee did nothing but set her a little on edge.

She dug in her purse for her cell phone and dialed Mark's number. The phone rang a couple of times before she heard her son's voice, caught in the middle of a laugh.

"Mom! Hey!"

The love in his tone warmed her and even brought a tear to her eye.

"How are you, *mi hijo*? Is everything going all right?"

"Yeah, Mom. I'm having a great time. Papa cooked me eggs with chorizo this morning."

"Good! Are you keeping your *abuelo* out of trouble?"

"Ha! He's getting me in trouble. He's already offered me a beer and a cigarette. We're out hunting for wild women now."

Her throat nearly closed up with shock. "What?" she gasped.

"Grandpa says I'm a man now, so it's time to get

initiated. I didn't know there was a whorehouse here."

Marisol blinked rapidly in disbelief. She could hardly believe what she was hearing. "Mark?"

As she floundered in flustered silence, waiting for the right words to come to her, she could hear her father in the background, his tone clearly one of reproof. Listening closer, she heard Mark's almost strangled laughter.

He had to be yanking her chain.

That little snot.

She bit back her first annoyed response. Two could play that game.

"All right, *querido*, but you make sure they give you the works for your first time, *si*? If your grandfather is paying for it, you might as well get the deluxe package."

Mark's turn for stunned silence. Marisol smirked at her own reflection in the rearview mirror. *Served him right. Cigarettes, alcohol, and a whorehouse, indeed.*

Finally he coughed a couple of times and returned to the conversation.

"All right, *Mamacita mia*, but Papa says you'll have to chip in for the extras."

She heard them both laughing now. *Jerks.* "Bring me a receipt, then."

"Will do. Oh, Papa says maybe we'll go up to the lake tomorrow night. They're having some kind of fishing contest."

"Catch a big one, then! I've got to go. Have fun."

Smiling as she clicked the phone shut, she inhaled another whiff of the delicious food. Whether Analisa, Teresa, and Penny waited inside or not, she was ready to start. She ran a quick comb through her hair and even smeared on a little lip gloss. After her encounter with Russell Asher, she definitely felt pretty again.

****

"And then she turned around and saw her skirt got tucked inside her underwear. You could see everything. Everything."

The four women in their brightly colored cotton summer dresses burst out in hysterical laughter. Those seated nearby turned to see what cracked them up. Marisol didn't care. For the first time in years she'd just let go, relaxed enough to stop worrying what others thought. Even here in her hometown, most of the people in the restaurant did not know her. She could do anything she wanted. Who would care?

Besides, if they discovered her alter ego was Jerrika Jones, she *could* do anything. She was nearly a celebrity, after all. Maybe not A-list, but certainly somewhere up there in the alphabet.

They caught up on each other's lives and shared gossip about as many of the reunion returnees they cared about. Penny, who worked at the hair salon where Tiffany Kearns' sister got her hair done, insisted on sharing the whole lowdown on what happened between Russell and Tiffany.

As Marisol listened to the tragic tale, a sense of indignation on Russell's behalf welled up in her, since it was clear Tiffany was the instigating party in the breakup. She was also surprised he hadn't acted more proactively. If Mark's father had tried to take him from her, Marisol would have gone nuclear on him. There was no way he could have won.

Although, it *was* the Kearns family. *Sometimes you just ran up against things you couldn't change.*

At the same time, she rationalized that it could all be attributed to karma. He dumped her for the purebred uptown girl; Tiffany dumped him for being as bi-racial as Marisol. Maybe that made them even.

After drinks and dinner, Analisa ordered a piece of strawberry cheesecake and four forks. Teresa and Penny whispered together, little giggles escaping their confab, until Marisol demanded to know what secret plan they were up to.

"Teresa, tell her," Analisa said, nudging her elbow.

"You're in on this, too?" Marisol asked with an accusatory look at her friend.

Teresa grinned. Her front teeth still jutted out, crooked, since her parents could not afford braces for her as a kid. She said it was why she now worked for the local radio station, where how she looked didn't matter. "A face meant for radio, isn't that what they always say?"

Clearing her throat, Teresa waited until she had the whole table's undivided attention, and leaned in close. "I want to interview you...Jerrika."

The three howled with laughter, drowning out the Muzak. People around them hardly looked up after the whole evening's worth of rowdy carrying-on.

Ana smiled at Marisol's gape of shock. "I had to tell them, *querida*. We're just so proud of you."

"We are!" Penny hurried to assure her. "Ana said you were ready to come out of the closet, you know, let everyone here know who you are and what you've done!" She hugged Marisol tight.

"So can I?" Teresa begged. "I've got the keys to the studio. We can go tonight after dinner. The interview can run in the morning on the talk show. And by the time you meet Russell at the dance tomorrow, everyone will know the truth. You'll be famous."

Marisol hesitated. She hadn't really intended to make a huge public announcement. But then...

She thought about the way Russell seemed to really appreciate that she wrote for a living, almost proud of the fact she'd been able to support herself and her son on her own. In Ocala, Mark had his circle of friends who didn't need to know who his mother was. Here? The only ones who mattered were her friends. Surely the announcement would be the right thing to do, an extra little homecoming boost for her ego.

She caught the infectious grin of the others and nodded. "All right. Let's do it!"

"You won't be sorry," Teresa promised. "And I'll have the big scoop of the whole reunion! I might even get a raise."

They toasted her potential raise with their water glasses and devoured the cheesecake, speculating about the faces of the others the next night as they discovered someone they'd never expected to meet. Jerrika Jones, the famous mommyblogger everyone would be talking about.

They all rode in Analisa's big SUV to the station, chattering about the old neighborhood and others of their class.

"I hope your interview goes ahead of the Select Choice winner," Teresa muttered as they pulled in. "The station manager likes me. I'll beg, if I have to."

"It's not such a big deal," Marisol said, but even as she spoke, she felt a burgeoning excitement grow in her. The idea really appealed to her, the more she considered it. Teresa had promised to make her a copy of the interview on CD so that she could take it home and let Mark hear it, too. *If he was even interested. It wasn't about cars or girls or school, so…*

"I'm going to make this happen."

Teresa unlocked the door and led them into the building, flipping on lights as she went. WLKE's worn hall carpet, once probably blue, had faded to a nondescript gray. The wood paneling certainly hailed from the 1970s, with its patina dulled into a flat plain brown. The place, however, entranced Marisol. She'd never stepped inside a radio studio in her life. Everything looked magical in her eyes.

The studio itself looked much more modern, shinier with equipment stacked everywhere. Teresa disappeared into a closet and clicked some switches, powering up the apparatus. *How did she ever learn to deal with all these electronics? It's all I can do to work my laptop and post things on social media. I'm impressed.*

"Can we sit in?" Penny asked, her eyes as wide and amazed as Marisol's.

"If you shut up, *querida*."

Teresa winked, taking any sting from her words. They all knew Penny often suffered from verbal diarrhea, even worse than Analisa. It was just her way.

"Fine." Penny rolled her eyes and perched on one of the tall stools at the table.

Teresa gestured to the other chairs, and Ana and Marisol hurried to sit down. She handed Marisol headphones and put on her own. A few more adjustments to the dials on the instrument board in front of her brought the lights to green. "Ready?" she asked.

Marisol's nerves made her giggle. "I guess." She

picked at a tissue from her pocket, leaving it in shreds on the table in front of her.

"All right, here we go." Teresa clicked the recording mechanism on.

"Good morning, West Exeter! This is Teresa White, with a special event for WLKE. As the class of 1985 comes back together to celebrate twenty years since graduating, a star has emerged. I am honored to be sitting in the WLKE studio with the one and only Jerrika Jones, the woman who has turned single motherhood into one heroic quest. Welcome, Jerrika."

A little startled to be addressed as her alter ego, Marisol stammered, "Thank you, Teresa."

Teresa grinned across the table at her. "Before we discuss your successful blog and career, perhaps our listeners would like to know your real name, and your connection to our little city."

Marisol took a deep breath. This was it.

"While I write as Jerrika, my name is Marisol Herrera Slade, and I'm a graduate of the class of 1985…"

Chapter Eight

Russell invited his old teammates Mike Johnson and Ham Berson to dinner at his parents' house Friday night. First, he wanted to see them, but second, he knew his mother's sense of Southern hospitality would keep her from bringing up the subject of his sons in front of company.

After the encounter in the park, he wanted to avoid that subject at any cost.

His friends showed up right on time, casual in light cotton shirts and relaxed-fit khakis, the uniform of the forty-something former jock. Mike still stood six feet two, but he'd bulked up so even his shadow imitated a hulk as he stood on the steps outside. He served as an officer in the county sheriff's office, second in command of the Marine Unit, Lake Patrol. Ham had gone the other way, looking almost gaunt, nearly bald. But his recent cancer treatments, not his age, caused that.

"Rusty, man!" Mike grabbed his shoulders and shook him hard enough to rattle his teeth. "How the hell are you?"

"Good, good," he said, laughing as he belatedly remembered the man's bear-like nature. He stepped out of reach. "I'm so glad you came."

Mike's grin spread across his face like a sunrise. "Are you kidding? I was always hot for your mother."

"Shut up!" Russell punched Mike in the arm.

Ham laughed. "She was fantasy material, man. And the best cook in town. Beat the hell out of my mom."

Russell barely had time to scowl before his mother came into the room behind them. "I heard that," she said. "I'm glad you boys appreciate my cooking as much as Rusty does."

Hoping that's all she heard, Russell closed the door behind his friends, feeling a little awkward now that they had grown into men instead of gangly athletes. *Men who had fantasized about my mother. Whoa.*

"How are you boys?" Kate asked. "All grown up with families of your own?"

"Yes, ma'am," they replied in unison.

"You'll have to tell me all about them. And I hope you brought pictures!"

"Of course," Mike said.

Kate grinned. "Rusty, you should have called Mike when we moved. He looks strong enough to have helped carry things." She studied both guests and patted Ham on the shoulder. "You look better."

Russell's eyebrow peaked in curiosity.

Ham's smile showed faint, but sincere. "I ran into your mom when she volunteered at the hospital. I saw her when I was getting my treatments."

"I made sure he got where he needed to be," she said. "I push a mean wheelchair."

"No one pops a wheelie like Kate Asher," Ham agreed.

Mike and Russell exchanged skeptical glances. Kate, flustered, ushered them into the kitchen to eat.

Joshua presided over the meal, as always, and

Russell could almost feel himself back in the day, on a Friday night, then three young men stoking their personal engines before an evening on the court. The conversation involved different topics now, of course: work, politics, and the state of the economy instead of grades and three-pointers. But the dynamics remained the same, and he saw his parents' pleasure at the interaction with "young people" in the sparkle of their eyes.

During dinner, several times his mind wandered from the delicious baked chicken and vegetables to the earlier meeting with Marisol Herrera. She seemed so normal, so quietly solid. She'd aged well, without Tiffy's need to resort to a bottle to keep her hair looking like it did when she was in high school.

He'd definitely gotten the feeling that Marisol still had feelings for him; the shy note in her voice while speaking to him, the way she couldn't always meet his eyes, these things let him know. He didn't quite understand how she could even be nice to him, considering their history; she was obviously a better person that he was. She'd never be like Tiffy and throw her single motherhood in a man's face.

As he considered their conversation, he regretted she lived in Florida. So far away. He'd been lonely after the divorce. Nothing much but casual dates. Hard to find someone with common interests. Harder to trust someone. He and Marisol didn't know the details of each other's lives well after all these years, of course, but the Internet and other modern conveniences made it easy to remedy that.

It sure would feel great to come home to someone again.

Besides, Marisol clearly understood a parent's love for a son, something Russell knew plenty about. He envied her close relationship with her boy. If only he could have the same with his own.

Would he really force Barret and Jon to go with him on Sunday? Could he? What would he do if they wouldn't go?

"Rusty?"

He blinked himself back to the room, away from his troubling thoughts, as his mother called him. "What?"

"Your father asked you about taking him to the country tomorrow afternoon." Her voice held mild reproof.

"Oh. Sorry, Dad. Woolgathering. I'm getting older. You know how it is."

His broad wink brought a laugh from the group, and he joined back in, setting Sunday aside to await its time. He had nearly two days. Surely he'd come up with an answer by then.

****

He woke up late Saturday—late for him, anyway. As district manager, he was required to be at work by seven a.m. six days a week. Sleeping till ten was a real luxury.

Waking up with the hangover from hell? Not quite so luxurious.

Groaning as he sat upright and the ache hit him full force, he grabbed his forehead with one hand and yanked the cord for the blinds with the other, making the room as dark as he could.

He still wore his clothes from the night before. Where had he and his friends gone? He pushed into the pain in his head and prodded his brain for information. They'd done tequila shots somewhere out by the lake, maybe Jerry's? Maybe the End of the Road. *Hell, maybe both.*

He remembered something about the Indians playing on the cable channel till Ham got too ticked off at Mitchell's pitching and threw a glass at the television. They got thrown out of wherever that had been.

Man. He was getting too old for this.

He stumbled down the hall to the bathroom, praying he wouldn't run into his parents. He really didn't need a lecture on the evils of drinking too much, not now. Thankfully, he heard nothing. They must be out for the morning.

He'd promised to take his dad somewhere… where the hell was it? Out to pick up some piece of lawn care equipment at a repair shop outside of town. That wasn't till afternoon, though. He was still okay. Just had to kick this hangover first.

He grabbed the bottle of ibuprofen from the medicine cabinet and carted it back to the bedroom. Fortunately, his mother decorated the spare room in bland white, tan, and beige, so no bright colors assaulted his recovering eyes. Plopping down on the bed, he groaned again as that jarred his head.

"Damn it. And I forgot water."

He popped the lid and poured four capsules into his hand, prepared to take them dry. He noticed for the first time a plate on the end table, with a stack of vitamin C chewables, a glass of tomato juice, and a note from his mother.

Bet you could use this. Don't forget you're taking

Dad at 1. Love you.

Russell couldn't decide if he was angry she assumed he'd need a hangover cure, or glad she'd acted thoughtfully. In the end, he shoved the ibuprofen in his mouth, chugged the juice, and crunched the round orange pills as a chaser, fighting a round of nausea.

He counted to ten, lay down, but quickly got up again. Nope, that wasn't going to solve it. His head spun when he lay horizontally. He needed distraction, something else to focus on. Maybe a round of his war game. Or some kind of video game, just something besides the pounding in his head.

But the boot-up seemed to take forever.

He tapped his right toe on the floor, waiting, waiting, counting to keep himself focused elsewhere besides on his interior.

He should know better. He DID know better. Ridiculous.

The reason lay with Tiffy. *But the fault was mine.*

Bits and pieces of the conversation came back to him. The guys had talked about Miss High-and-Mighty Tiffany and her family, and his sons. His sons, who even Ham saw more often than Russell did, since he still lived in town. Russell had gotten more and more frustrated and rinsed his ire thoroughly with alcohol. He'd been determined to numb his senses at the time.

Not so much now.

Maybe some music. He reached over to the bedside table and turned on the small alarm-clock radio there, fumbling for the switch to turn it to the FM band. His hand stopped when he heard a familiar voice.

Was that Marisol?

Two women were talking about the Internet, and

that horrid Jerrika Jones. He couldn't move, drawn in like a moth to a light source. That *was* Marisol, and Teresa… oh, what was her name… the one with teeth like that cartoon bunny.

"Being a single mother can't be easy, Marisol. How has your writing helped you be a better parent?"

"I find a lot of support from other women—and men—who read my blog. We share tips on how to save money, how to deal with kids of every age, where good bargains can be found. I even have one subscriber who's a family law attorney who answers questions every so often on legal issues, you know, general things, since each state is different. It's a great group. I'm very blessed."

Russell's fogged brain snapped a little closer to focus. So Marisol blogged, too? He'd have to show her his own blog. She'd understand his feelings about Tiffany and his boys then. Surely she would. He turned up the radio just a little.

"What does your son think of his mother, now that she's famous?" Teresa asked.

Marisol laughed softly. "Oh, I don't know if his opinion has changed so much. He still complains when I make him clean his room and take out the trash."

Russell wondered idly if Jon and Barret did any chores around the house. He sincerely doubted it. Tiffany likely employed a maid and a lawn boy for her mini-mansion on Lake Shore Drive, like her parents did. Heaven forbid housework got in the way of her boys' tennis lessons or $100 haircuts.

He suddenly hoped they wouldn't grow up as useless and shallow as their mother.

He must do something about that. As soon as

possible.

One of the women said "Jerrika," and that yanked his attention back to the radio again. Why were they still talking about that woman?

"I'm not really sure why I chose that name, particularly," Marisol was saying. "Jerrika Jones seemed like a really strong name. Someone who knew what she was doing. Someone people would listen to. So far, that's turned out to be right."

"As someone who's known you for years, Marisol, I've got to say that being Jerrika has brought you a long way. I see those same qualities in you. Someone who's confident and strong. You've done a great job raising your son on your own. You've got a lot to be proud of."

"Thank you."

Russell could hear the shy blush in Marisol's response, but what he heard more was the roar of his own blood pressure pounding in his ears. What? Had he heard that right? Marisol Herrera was… Jerrika Jones?

He shoved his laptop aside with a muttered curse. "Arrggh!" The revelation had raised his blood pressure. That exacerbated the headache. Maybe he'd be all right if he just stroked out about then.

How could that sweet, nice, supportive woman he sat and drank coffee with the day before be the same one who dealt verbal blows to so-called "deadbeat dads" in that blog column Stuart was always raging about?

His eyes widened. *Stuart.*

He wondered if perhaps Stuart had heard the broadcast as well. If so, he'd likely be on the warpath. After all the blazing written exchanges he'd shared with that man-hater, he'd sworn he would knock Jerrika flat on her can if he ever met her face to face.

And they'd all be together at the dance that night.

The interview wrapped up and Teresa signed off. The station moved on to a national news report as the half hour hit, but he couldn't stop thinking about her.

He wondered if he should contact her—somehow. It's not like he'd asked for her number. But it didn't seem fair somehow to let her be ambushed like that. *Just in case she really was as amiable as she appeared to be then.*

He looked up the number for the radio station and dialed it; it just rang through to an answering machine. *Maybe Saturday is just pre-programmed stuff. I'll try to get to the dance a little early. Just to keep an eye on things.*

He headed for the shower. Tonight was going to be an interesting one.

Chapter Nine

The next morning, Analisa insisted on a run to the outlet mall at Grove City to catch the uber-sale at her favorite bath products store.

Marisol loved the products from that store but couldn't often afford them. Certainly not now when she must corral every penny to make sure Mark's school bills would get paid. Even if the school and grants paid his tuition, and part of his room and board, many other expenses like books and fees still came due. When she'd filled out the application for financial aid and compared it against the "anticipated cost of college" document they'd received from the university…well, it had taken her breath away.

Mark had saved, too, and he assured her they could do it—together.

But that left her very little to spend, especially after the cost of the trip to the reunion.

Ana talked her into tagging along anyway.

"You've got a big date tonight," Ana teased as they headed south on the interstate.

"It's not a date."

Marisol hadn't stopped thinking about her meeting with Russell the day before, how his voice still stirred up her insides, even after all these years. In high school, she'd done stupid little things to try to reclaim his attention, like making signs to hold up at basketball games, or always finding herself in the hall where his locker was located. But she was past that now.

She thought she was.

Maybe.

She stared out the open window, as a warm breeze caressed her face.

Summer in the north spread forth as green, lush, and beautiful as Marisol remembered it, the thick emerald leaves of oaks and maples far more all-encompassing in the landscape than the scanty coconut palms and tropical flower bushes back home. Today was a Chamber of Commerce kind of day, too, the azure sky puffy with bright white cumulus clouds, and sunlight bringing everything to the height of its color. She missed these summers.

Then there was that other half of the year. The frozen part. Living near the Great Lakes in the winter was even less than no picnic. It was icy hell. She'd keep the tropics, and her life there, thank you very much.

"You know," she said. "I did have some pins made up with Jerrika's toon, and the Web site and all. Business cards, too."

"What? Give me one of those pins right now!"

"You're driving."

"Duh. Really? I can put on a pin while I'm driving!"

Marisol frowned. "No, you can't."

"Dare me?" Ana's chubby hand reached across from the driver's seat. "Gimme."

"I didn't come all the way to Pennsylvania to die on Interstate 79." Marisol's lips formed a stubborn line. "When we get there."

"Fine. *Gilí.*"

75

"All that education, and you have to call me a dummy. Makes me glad I skipped college. I can insult you just as well, and I don't have the student loans to pay back."

"That's cold, Mari. Really cold."

Satisfied she'd made her point, Marisol settled into the seat and returned to looking out the window.

Had Russell heard the morning interview? She and Ana had listened as they'd finished getting dressed for their trip to the mall. Marisol thought she'd sounded competent and professional. She couldn't wait until the dance to see how her former classmates would react to the news.

When they arrived at Grove City, Ana took the button from Marisol but kept hold of her hand. A very serious look set on her face.

"What?" Marisol guessed whatever Ana wanted to say must be unpleasant, or at least distasteful, because of the way she bit her lip.

"*Maricita*, I want you to have a wonderful time tonight. If what you want is to be able to hold your own with Russell Asher, then I want that for you, too."

She gestured toward her purse. "I thawed all my plastic out of the ice tray. Because you are my friend, I want you to let me buy you something incredible to wear tonight, something to make them all know you are truly, through and through, Miss Jerrika Jones, feminista."

Marisol didn't know whether to laugh or cry. She did the first till she did the second. "Feminista? Really?" The thought made her laugh harder.

"Hell, yes. You need something with attitude, *amiga*, and I want to buy it for you."

Ana's smile was so sincere, Marisol wished she could let her do that. But her pride stung at the thought that what she had wasn't good enough. She'd bought a few new things for the trip. Most of her clothing was in good shape, some of it even designer label, but purchased at consignment stores, not off the designer rack.

"Ana, I don't think so."

"*No discuta!* I'm going to buy the outfit, whether you wear it or not." She looked down at her own ample form. "And you know it won't fit me."

Torn between her pride and her desire to be that woman with attitude, Marisol sighed. "All right," she finally said. "But I'll pay you back."

"Write about me in your blog, *chica.* Then I can be famous, too."

That was a small enough request, Marisol thought. Wouldn't cost her much, and Ana would score a lot of points with her co-workers. "I'll still pay you back," she insisted.

Ana grinned and hugged her. "Then let's shop."

She pinned on the Jerrika Jones pin and urged Marisol to do the same. "Be bold, *mujer de mi corazón.*"

The next three hours were a whirl of trying on clothes and shoes and searching for accessories to match. Ana insisted the best outfit they found was a close assemblage of pieces copying Madonna's outfit from the movie *Desperately Seeking Susan,* which they'd all defied their parents to go see back in 1985. A cropped black-knit top, tight black pants, a shiny brown jacket with animal print lapels; all this topped by a tangle of silver and black necklaces, and finished with sharp mid-heel, low-cut black boots.

"I'll do your hair just like hers, with a black scarf tied in," Ana said, admiring over Marisol's shoulder in the dressing room mirror. "If only you were blonde. Hey…"

"No! I am not going blonde!"

"Oh, yeah. One nasty blonde in town's enough." Ana grinned. "All right. Take it all off again."

"What are you wearing?" Marisol worried, reaching for the boot buckle.

"Me? Eh. What I always wear. Polyester. I've got some chunky belts, though, and I'll layer those on." She shrugged. "No point in anyone looking at me, is there? You're the one who'll be the star."

The dressing room attendant knocked and peeked in. "Oh my gosh! You're channeling the Material Girl, right?" She studied Marisol a minute. "Wait right there. You're not quite perfect."

She vanished, leaving Ana and Marisol to exchange puzzled looks.

"You looked good to me." Ana leaned back against the wall of the changing room.

"Here!" The saleswoman opened the door and handed Marisol some square-framed sunglasses. "Try those."

Marisol slipped them on and looked in the mirror. With her hair up… She scooped her hair into her hand and held it at her crown, where the ends dangled appealingly. That was it. A snappy chick with style and attitude.

Jerrika lived and breathed.

"Perfect!" Analisa clapped her hands. "We'll take it all."

The woman waited while Marisol removed every piece, and disappeared to ring it up.

"You really shouldn't do this," Marisol said.

"Nonsense. I'd love to buy that for myself, but I don't look good in anything. It's my fashion plate doll fix for the month, *chica*. Let me enjoy it vicariously, hmm?"

Ana hugged her and followed the saleswoman out. Marisol dressed again in her secondhand threads, a final look in the mirror convincing her the jeans and slim T-shirt with a print vest wasn't terrible, just not new. By the time she got out to the register, Analisa had all the purchases stuffed into a big bag.

"You're going to have a night you won't forget, my friend," Ana promised as they headed back to the car.

****

"Do you think I'm being an idiot?"

Marisol and Ana sat on the nurse's tiny back porch, overlooking her unmowed yard. Each held a glass of spiced tea with cactus-shaped ice cubes. Ana had a whole cabinet full of plastic and silicone ice cube trays that made ice in all sorts of festive shapes. Marisol had resolved to sneak a couple into her luggage for the drive home.

"An idiot?" Ana shrugged. "Who's to say what makes someone an idiot? Trying the same thing twice and expecting a different result?" She winked. "I get it. Rusty is a good-looking man, who's single, and you have memories of good times together."

"But I have memories of horrible times, too. When he dumped me. Even though I didn't know it was for Tiffany Kearns at the time, it became pretty damned obvious. I should be cheering what she did as karma!"

Ana sipped her tea and nodded. "Certainly, it is. But word around town is that she's really screwing him over, especially with their sons."

Marisol had already shared what she saw at the park downtown. Analisa confirmed that was the usual scenario.

"She brought one of the boys into the ER for a sprained ankle several months ago and wouldn't let the staff there call the father. She waved her name around and threatened to have her father withdraw his support for the hospital charity drive if they did."

"What a—witch." Marisol frowned and pondered that. Unfortunately, it just made her feel sorrier for Rusty than she already did. *Poor guy. Even if you deserve some payback, that's you, personally, not your kids. They deserve a good relationship with their father.*

Even if he made stupid decisions.

"Besides," Ana said, "it's not like meeting him at the dance is asking him to marry you. You can't tell me you didn't want to see him again and flaunt how well you survived his dumping you. I mean, I'm sure you didn't come all this way just to see me."

"Ana! Of course I wanted to see you. Don't be silly." She inadvertently gestured with her iced tea and spilled some of it on the stones below.

"And?"

Ana wasn't going to let her off the hook, apparently.

"Oh, all right, and I wanted to see what had happened with him. Now that he's single... who knows?"

"Exactly. Who knows? You are going to look

fantastic and make a big dent in his heart large enough to let the right choice in! I can't wait to see his face!"

But fate scuttled Ana's plans. Just as they were getting ready to leave for dinner, she got called into work. Try as she might to convince the shift nurse she had more important things to do—once in a lifetime things to do!—she couldn't wrench success from her efforts.

She sighed and went to change out of her 80s finery. When she came back out in uniform, she grabbed her keys.

"They promised I'll be out in time to hit the dance by ten. A couple of the nurses were in a car wreck this afternoon and are actually patients instead of working tonight. So the hospital just needs coverage till the night shift comes in as scheduled."

"That's wrong in so many ways." Marisol sympathized.

"You get all dolled up. I can't wait to see you when I get there." Analisa headed for the door. "Russell Asher will be beside himself."

Marisol laughed, a little nervous hiccup. "I hope so. See you there."

Alone, she didn't have the motivation to go out to dinner, so she dug through Analisa's cupboards and found some cinnamon cereal that satisfied her just fine. Her nerves ate at her. Announcing her alter ego to the public had pushed her comfort zone, despite her best intentions. She didn't regret the interview, but preparing to meet her public scared her all the same. Hiding behind Jerrika provided its advantages.

The dance started at eight, and she and Ana had agreed to meet Teresa and Penny there. With a couple of hours to kill, she took the time to walk the old neighborhood, listening to the kids yell and the babies cry, just like when she and her family lived here. She walked down Agnes Lane, all the way to the end, standing a moment, arms crossed tight, as she studied the house where she'd grown up.

The gray wood-framed house seemed even smaller than she remembered, and she wondered whether it could really accommodate three bedrooms inside. Marisol had shared her room with two older sisters, her brothers had the second, and her parents took the small third, barely larger than a walk-in closet. The family shared one bathroom, a nightmare on school mornings, and the tiny kitchen didn't even hold a table. Everyone just grabbed a plate and found somewhere to perch long enough to eat.

The house looked abandoned now. Old junk sat piled in the yard, but it didn't look like anyone had touched it for a long time. Marisol was tempted to sneak up and peek in the windows, but at the same time, thought it would just make her sad. She kept walking.

Her family hadn't been the same after Mama died. That occurred the same summer she'd gambled on Russell Asher and lost. Her sisters had both left the house by then, one married with two babies and the other working as a waitress in Syracuse. Her brothers stayed with Papa after, but not long. They'd gone out west, somewhere. None of them had heard from Pepito for a couple of years now. She hoped he wasn't dead. Johnny worked construction, floating here and there following available work. He sent an occasional post card, and they read and reread each before placing it on the refrigerator door to treasure.

She knew that made her father sad. He and Mama had given up the migrant life, renting the house here in West Exeter purposefully so their children could grow up in a community, so they'd have roots. Yet they'd all moved away anyway.

But roots were important. That lesson she'd learned, and made sure Mark learned as well. Hard enough for a boy to grow up without a father. She'd landed in Ocala and stayed put most of his life, so he'd have friends and neighbors to care about him.

She walked in the other direction, back toward the small stores, run by the same families who owned them when she was a girl. Probably the kids she'd known served as the proprietors now. Thinking of Santino and Dressa working behind the counter proved a real eye-opener. Where had all the time gone?

As dusk started to fall, Marisol reluctantly gave up her little trip down memory lane and returned to Ana's house to dress. The outfit seemed more like a costume now, without Ana's enthusiasm to spur her on. But when she added the sunglasses, she knew she would make a splash.

Now to cultivate a bit of Jerrika's sass and vinegar… She struck a pose to make even Madonna proud.

"Vogue," she whispered, holding one hand in front of her face.

She locked the door behind her and headed for her car. "Look out, Wright High, here I come," she said as she pulled out and drove toward town.

Chapter Ten

Russell arrived fifteen minutes late to the high school, having to park in the outermost area of the lot. *Kind of like every day when I was a student. I never could get out of bed in time to make the front row.* Laughing at himself, he straightened his pink zebra-striped blazer. The black slacks and black T-shirt he already had. *Made shopping for a costume pretty easy.* He snapped on his shades and headed in.

The décor reflected early high-school gym, plenty of draped, colored crepe paper and paper balls. He remembered several dances in his high-school career looking pretty much the same. The bass pounded, echoing off the walls and managing to drown out, somehow, the chatter of a hundred voices.

As he paused on the threshold, Michael Jackson's "Thriller" started to play. With a roar of approval, men and women alike scrambled to the dance floor as the strobe lights flashed. They posed and jerked in the center of the dance floor, performing their best zombie impressions to the catchy beat of the music.

He surveyed the crowd, checking out the '80s garb. Man, some of those outfits really took him back. *And we think the kids of today look wild and crazy.*

A good number of the attendees clustered around the bar at the far end of the room. *Seems like a good place to begin.*

He strolled over, trying to ignore Debbie's strident summons from the front, calling him, no doubt to hear his plan for the "Tequila" dance. He'd rather immerse himself in something tall and cold.

He ordered from the white-jacketed bartender and leaned up against the bar, studying the room.

Marty Drogan, ostentatiously visible in an outsized green Hawaiian shirt, crossed the room, his hips swaying in a manner Russell guessed Marty imagined to be sexy. He raised a crystal mixed-drink glass in Russell's direction. "Tequila!" he yelled.

"Ah, yes. 'Tequila,' " Russell answered, rolling his eyes as he turned back to the bartender, who held his drink. He paid for the beer and moved to the end of the bar where he could see the crowd and the door. He hadn't been able to reach Marisol—or should he say Jerrika Jones?—to just give a heads-up about a possible reaction from Stuart.

You're probably worrying about nothing. Stu is a lot of things, but he's not insane. He won't start anything in this public setting.

Right?

Unfortunately, he wasn't sure of this at all. He scanned the crowd, trying to spot either of them, but it was hard to identify people in their costumes.

He took a long drink and raised his glass to Mike, who'd just moseyed through the door, his wife a step behind him. Mike, unlike Russell, apparently resisted the temptation to dress retro style. He wore a blue plaid cotton shirt and a standard pair of mall-bought jeans.

The little woman—what was her name again? Sally? Susie?—wore a soft floral dress. She did not graduate in their class. Mike met the petite blonde in college, waiting outside Madison Square Garden for the Big East Tournament when Susie and her girlfriend came past costumed in Star Trek gear, complete with pointy ears. A closet Trekker, Mike discovered love at first sight.

"Rusty!" Mike bellowed over the music, which switched to "Easy Lover." Phil Collins. Ugh. *When are they getting to the hair bands? Now that was real 80s music.*

Several people delayed Mike's progress as he made his way toward the bar, and Susie stayed a step behind him all the way. Russell ordered a second Heiney, and got one for Mike, too. He didn't know what the wife drank. Mike could handle that.

More people came in, none of them Jerrika. He overheard the name, though, several times from little conversation knots of people as the minutes ticked by. Obviously a lot of people heard the broadcast this morning. They acted a lot more impressed than he.

"Is she here yet?" Susie asked Russell.

"Who?"

"Jerrika! What's her name, honey?"

"Marisol Herrera." Mike reached for the tall beer glass Russell held out to him. "You seen her, Russ? You said you talked to her yesterday afternoon."

"Haven't seen her."

"Man, I can't believe she's someone famous now. She was so quiet back in school. She had the jones for you, though. Oh, hell yes."

"Russell was probably everyone's crush, wasn't he?" Susie grinned at her husband's friend. "He's pretty cute."

Mike didn't even give her a look. "Oh yeah, he's

the man, all right."

Debbie, a thick pad of paper on a clipboard before her, took the mic as the song ended and announced, "All right, everyone, get a drink to cool off and stay focused. Russell Asher's going to judge our Tequila Big Shoe dance in ten minutes. Right, Russell?"

"You betcha," Russell called out, reluctant to release his foreboding mood. But the small round of applause that followed cheered him up a little. Even if Tiffany had no need for him, other people did. That was nice.

He leaned his back against the bar, checking out the crowd. He identified about half of the people there as from his class. Name tags helped, of course. Some of the people he'd never recognize without those little white tags, they'd changed so much. Most changes involved the usual over twenty years: a little heavier, a little grayer.

He leafed through the twelve-page booklet organizers compiled with everyone's name and a biographical paragraph telling what each graduate accomplished since high school. Out of the class of two hundred and fifty, nearly twenty had died; three who worked at the World Trade Center and perished in the terrorist attacks in 2001. Others died fighting in the wars in the Middle East. A couple had gotten involved in meth rings, which most people wrote off as self-induced.

Not everything involved bad news. Several grads evolved into successful executives across the country, two on the west coast working on the cutting edge of computer development. Sammy Lynn Sanders succeeded as a rock star of sorts, not a bad gig for one of the bad girls. Most stayed in the area, working in the same industries as their fathers and mothers, a lot of them in tool and die. When he considered it, that might have been the smart move. A lot of those folks were making close to six figures and never spent a day in college.

Yeah, but I'm not doing so bad. At least, career-wise.

A couple of grads improved over the intervening time, of course. Frank Letman worked for the local police force and looked a lot less like the gangly boy they'd all called "Pizzaface." Shannon Walton lost about a hundred pounds and now snuggled at the center of an admiring group of men at a table over by the DJ.

And then there was Stuart.

Russell reflected on the angry post Stuart had penned on his blog after their earlier conversation:

How clever of you, oh-so-superior Jerrika, to point fingers and pontificate on the Internet. Since personal attack is your style, let me point out that not all men run out on their kids. Some of them are driven away by ball-busting bitches like you. No wonder your kid doesn't have a dad, and you've chosen a village of no-names to make up for the one thing your boy probably needed most: his father. You can't even be honest about who you really are. Great example for your kid.

"Rusty?" A voice spoke close to his ear, and he startled back to the present. Mike elbowed his ribs. "They're calling you, man."

"Oh, okay."

Russell looked around and saw faces oriented in his direction, someone up at the DJ's table beckoning him forward. "Must be 'Tequila' Time." He drained his glass and headed over.

"Sorry, Debbie," he said to the woman who waited patiently there for him. "Preoccupied."

"You promised," she said, her brow furrowed and a slight scold to her tone. She gestured to the DJ, asking him to cue up the song. She grabbed the microphone. "All right, everyone, get ready to dance!"

Feeling a little ridiculous and wondering why he'd let her talk him into this, Russell took the spot right in front of the table, others filling in around him as he pointed his fingers in imitation of Pee Wee Herman's performance. What the hell, right? What's the worst he could do, make a fool of himself?

In this town, he'd already done that plenty.

Why stop now?

Some of the dancers were seriously overtop with their performances. He tried hard not to laugh out loud. What he really needed to do was get up on the bleachers and check out the dancers at a better angle.

He maneuvered his way through the crowd until he was up on the third level, where he had a birds-eye view of the group. Not only could he see the Pee-Wee dancers, he also spotted Stuart coming in the double doors. He hadn't dressed for the occasion, like Mike. His face was red, and his body language showed anxiety practically dripping off him. He glanced around the room, growing more agitated the longer he stood there.

If I can't warn Marisol, I should at least tell Mike or Frank. Someone should be aware that there could be a 'scene.'

Or that a scene might be the least of it.

Stuart was angry, that much Rusty knew, but he

couldn't imagine he'd get violent. All the same, a yelling match would do nothing to add to the attendees' good times this evening.

While he considered the consequences, he lost focus. When he looked at the doorway again, Stuart was gone.

The music stopped, and the dancers gave a roar of applause, congratulating themselves for letting their hair down. *At least what was left of it.* He quickly pointed out the couple he thought achieved the spirit of 'Tequila' best to Debbie, and escaped back into the crowd, looking for Stuart.

The buzz of conversation grew louder—or was that only his imagination? Tension inched up his neck like a boa constrictor, driving the blood to pounding in his head. He caught a glimpse of Mike, finally, and made his way through the sea of people until he was close enough to speak without yelling.

"Hey, Mike, we might have a problem here. Have you seen Stuart Fry tonight?"

"Stuart? Umm, I might have. Did you check the bar?"

"Not yet. Look, he's kind of heated about Marisol—Jerrika Jones. The two of them have been trading barbs on blogs about single parenthood. Considering some things he's said…"

He wondered how much he could really say without feeling like he was betraying his friend.

"Considering? Like what? Has he made threats?"

Russell hesitated, then nodded.

Mike sighed. "Great. Just what we need tonight. Does Marisol know?"

"I don't think so."

"All right. Thanks for the alert." He hitched up his pants. "Be right back, Susie." He meandered through the crowd, headed for the door.

Susie pouted. "Work, work, work. No matter where we go, something always pops up." Her pout faded into a wicked smile. "But maybe I can have a couple drinks while he's gone." She patted Russell's arm and sidled up to the bar.

I wonder what that's about. But you know what? I don't want to know. I already know too damn much.

He got another beer and kept patrolling, on the lookout now for Marisol. He imagined she'd look pretty much like she had at the restaurant—a quiet wallflower, blending into the crowd. She never gave a fig for having all the latest fashion trends. Just like him, why start something new just for this occasion?

Chapter Eleven

I'm glamorous. Who'd have believed it?
Soaking in the heady attraction of being dressed up, excited at the prospect of meeting her old classmates on this new level, and anticipating perhaps her last chance at reconnecting with Russell, she thought she could just float to the school rather than drive.

She parked her car in the lot at the high school, a new experience for her, as she'd never had a car in school. Coming in, she'd driven along the road that hugged the lake, admiring the view.

People played at the water's edge, but not many swam. Pymatuning was a pretty lake, most of it a state park, but even by summer's end it wasn't warm by her Florida standards. The water didn't flaunt the pretty blue-green of Florida waters, either, but a dull gray-blue. On stormy days, she recalled, the water whipped up frothy whitecaps on steel gray, reflecting the dark clouds overhead.

At least from the shore, it appeared beautiful.

Maybe before she went home, her father could take her, with Mark, out for a ride on his small boat.

A smile came to her as she thought about her school years here and how they all clamored for a chance to run and dip into those chill waters during vacation, those opportunities coming less frequently as high school progressed and work intruded into leisure time.

But now she was her own boss. And she was here to celebrate that.

Shutting out feelings of inadequacy formerly haunting her in these halls, she walked up to the front door of the school, which was decorated with bright foil letters celebrating the reunion events.

Several whistles came her direction, and her walk became a little strut. She cultivated more confidence on the boots' heels, an unaccustomed height for her. She imagined herself as Jerrika, or even Madonna herself, and mentally set herself to make a grand entrance.

Gloria Estefan's "Conga" blasted down the hall into the lobby, cluing her in to her destination. The rhythm seemed to sink right into her bones, her heritage and years in Florida giving her great appreciation for the music of the Miami Sound Machine. Her hips moved in response. This was her element; she was flying.

In the room, she saw she wasn't the only one. A long conga line snaked among the tables, picking up new dancers as it moved along, everyone singing along. She watched from the doorway, amazed, delight pulling up the corners of her mouth into a huge smile.

Teresa and Penny appeared from the crowd and ran over to grab Marisol's hand. "Come on! This is our song!"

They dragged her to the tail end of the line, and the three of them clutched on, lost in the rhythm. The conga line bent and twisted, and the faces passed dizzily by as the music took over. When the song ended, whoops and clapping followed, and the dancers broke up, returning to their seats.

Marisol realized she still wore her dark glasses and slipped them off. With a flash of shy excitement she found she was the subject of a lot of stares from the crowd.

"You look fantastic!" Teresa whispered in her ear. "If your hair was bleached, I'd think—"

"I'm not blonde. Will not be. Ever."

Marisol bit back her annoyance, knowing her friend was just trying to be helpful.

But why would she want to remind herself of the one thing that had come between her and Russell Asher? Not much percentage in that, now, was there?

"Sorry." Teresa pouted a minute, then pointed to the lapel of her short dark jacket. "Look, I'm wearing your pin!"

Jerrika's cartooned appearance did in fact reside on Teresa's jacket, as it did on Penny and Marisol's as well. She'd brought more pins in her pocket, just in case anyone else asked for one. Maybe she was being a little prideful, thinking anyone would care about her enough to ask. But common practice among those who hoped to be "someone" meant self-promotion. It was an uncomfortable reality she'd had to come to terms with. Since she wanted to play the game, it behooved her to play by the rules.

"Has anyone said anything about the interview?" Marisol asked, idly glancing around the room to see if Russell had really come. She'd half wondered if he'd ditch the informal dance for the more formal event at the West Exeter Club, black tie and all, once he'd thought about his choices. Something more in line with his social stature.

But he'd said he would be here.

"Sure," Teresa said, making her way to the table stocked with crudités and chips. "The station manager was thrilled and gave me two more interview assignments. This might have been my big break, Mari. Thank you so much!"

"That's great."

Teresa loaded up a plate, but Marisol was too consumed with nervous butterflies beating inside her ribs to think about food. Where was Russell?

"O.M.G., you must be Jerrika. I just *love* you!" gushed a woman who got up from a table nearby to come over and grasp Marisol's hand. "I'm Sandy. Men are scum, don't you think?"

"I— I'm glad you like the column, Sandy," Marisol stammered, startled.

"Jess. *Jess!*" The woman called to a polyester-suited woman at another table. "It's her!"

"It's who? That's Marisol Herrera. Oh, right! Your heroine." The other woman laughed and made her way through the crowd to shake Marisol's hand as well.

Marisol lost track of time over the next half hour as a parade of people came up to her, some of them familiar, others strangers, all of whom shared some connection to her story of single motherhood and its pitfalls and triumphs. She ended up passing out all the pins she brought. Teresa took a list of names for people who wanted one after she ran out.

"Send me a box at the station, Mari, and I'll get them distributed," Penny promised.

A little light-headed at the attention, Marisol could only nod. "Some water?" she asked, her knees a little weak.

A voice came from behind her shoulder. "Here, maybe this will suit you. Hemlock, isn't that more appropriate?"

Marisol blinked as a tall, balding guy appeared in front of her with a glass in his hand. He held it out to her. It looked like water, but the tone of his voice and the dark fury in his eyes made her wonder.

"I'm sorry. Do I know you?" She looked for a nametag, but he had nothing on his shirt that would identify him.

"I guess the question would be, do any of us know *you*? Hiding behind a fake name, taking potshots at dads who are out there trying to do their best. I mean, where do you get off, lady?"

His voice had started out conversational-level but gradually got louder. The people around them fell silent, the tension between the two almost solid as a wall.

"I can't believe people fall for that act," Stuart said. "Russell always said you were Little Miss Sweet Innocence, when this is who you are."

Aware of the attention focused on them, she wanted to fall through the floor. *I should have guessed that I wouldn't appeal to everyone...why did I ever do that interview?* Dios mio*, I was a fool. I should have just kept quiet. Maybe I shouldn't even have come at all.*

I definitely need some air. Pulling together as much of Jerrika as she could manage, she turned on her heel and walked away from him.

But he wouldn't let her.

She hadn't retreated fifteen feet when he followed and grabbed her arm, his fingers pinching, hurting her, and yanked her around to face him. His eyes, hot like melted steel, glared as if he wished he could shoot laser beams from them.

"No, no, you've got this coming to you. You and all the other women who think kids don't need their dads. You brag about how you're so superior, so wonderful, so everything that a man isn't. If you're so good, why don't you just have children on your own, since you don't need men? Don't just use us and toss us aside!"

Marisol's jaw dropped open, the unprovoked attack leaving her speechless. She stumbled on her boot heels, caught off guard by the depth of ferocity in every aspect of his being.

Someone caught her other arm to keep her from falling. "Hey, Stu, lay off," Russell said.

She'd never been so happy to see someone in her life. And he'd come to her rescue just like that knight on a horse.

Russell moved forward and stepped between them. "Look, I know you've got a beef with the character she writes, Stu, but this isn't that character. This is Mari. We went to school with her. You remember—"

"Get out of my way, Rusty. This one is gonna get what she deserves." Stu's nostrils flared, and his chest heaved with the breaths he was taking. Marisol actually thought he might have a stroke or a heart attack, he was so wound up. She couldn't remember meeting this guy at all, even when she'd heard his name was Stuart. She could hardly remember her own name. Certainly not in her current state of shock.

Another man stepped up behind Stuart, even taller. Marisol thought he vaguely resembled one of Rusty's teammates from basketball. What was his name? Mike something?

"Fry? Man, what are you doing? Let the woman go."

"Hey, this is between us. Butt out, pal." He growled, but he released her. She tripped backward in the damn heels, but Teresa caught her other elbow and kept her from falling.

"Afraid I can't do that. You're making an ass of yourself, that's what you're doing, my friend," the other man said. He glanced over his shoulder at the silent crowd watching the confrontation. "Nothing to see here, folks. Move along."

Mike pointed a finger at the DJ, who dialed up the digital player and Starship's "We Built This City" blared from the speakers a moment later. People started to drift back to the dance floor.

"Are you all right?" Teresa asked in a hushed voice, close to Marisol's ear.

Tears welled over from Marisol's eyes, partly at the receding pain in her arm, partly at the burning shame at such a public confrontation, and she wiped them away with the back of her gloved hand. All her tender self-esteem folded, threatened to vanish under the assorted hostile, curious, and startled stares.

The guy who'd interceded for her chased the gawkers off to other pursuits and tried to get Stuart to come away with him. Stuart, on the other hand, appeared as glued to the spot as Marisol.

"Keep your hands to yourself, all right, man? I don't want to have to take you in."

The other man's voice, mild on the surface, carried the strength of iron underneath. Marisol could see in

Stuart's eyes that he didn't want to back off. He still steamed on the inside. But he finally nodded and jammed his hands in his pockets, then walked away.

The man's words echoed and echoed in her head as she stood, frozen, grateful Teresa held her up so she didn't collapse.

The tears kept streaming, despite Marisol's best efforts to stanch the flow. Teresa urged her to come away, but she couldn't move, nailed to her spot. Russell still remained there by her side, though he didn't intervene further. What should she do?

She turned to Russell. "Thank you. If you hadn't shown up…"

He shrugged halfheartedly. "I mean, I don't totally disagree with him. You are kind of hard on dads. Hard enough to cause some damage. Is it really so much fun playing those games?"

Marisol, blindsided, fought to come up with a reply. Where was this coming from? She'd thought he approved of her writing career. She hadn't told him about Jerrika, but who'd have thought he even knew about the blog?

"Are you FreeDad91?" she asked, sudden understanding flowing through her.

"No. That's Stuart, though. I've probably sent a couple of replies to you when I feel particularly skewered by something you've said." He jerked, his face hurt for a moment, but recovered.

Unable to bear those who were still staring, Marisol whispered, "Can we go outside? Please?"

"What's going on here?" Marisol's friend Penny stepped up to Teresa's side, bright, dark eyes flicking like a sparrow's, studying each of them in turn.

"Someone said there was a fight?"

"Some jerk thought Mari had attacked him personally. God knows what he thought he was going to do. Mike got him out of here." Teresa frowned. "Come on, Mari. Let's go have fun."

Marisol watched Russell, her muscles slowly loosening, relaxing a little. Even if he was angry with Jerrika, she believed she could get through to him, if he'd just talk to her, away from all these people, in a place where he could let himself go. His hostility wasn't aimed at her, Marisol, but at Jerrika. Maybe she could help him separate the two once again.

"Go on, Teresita. I'll be along in a minute."

"Mari, no. I'm not leaving you." Teresa put her hands on her hips. "And I don't think you should go anywhere alone, if people are ready to punch your lights out for being someone with an opinion."

"I won't be alone. Just Rusty and me, outside," she said softly, in a soothing tone she might have used with an injured dog or cat. Or boy. Her eyes didn't leave Russell's.

He seemed to pull himself together and nodded once. "Maybe that's best."

"Marisol." Penny frowned. "Be careful."

Marisol wasn't worried about being careful. She worried about being the one to add insult to Tiffany's injury. Glancing around, she spied a back door. "Let's go out here."

For the moments it took to turn her back on Russell and wait for him to follow her outside, she depended on the strength of whatever of Jerrika resided inside her. She wanted a chance to explain, a chance to talk about Mark's father, a very different case from Russell and

Tiffany. She'd hurt him, unintentionally. *Or maybe there was some intentionality regarding single dads in general. I recall a little gloating in some of the columns.*

Make it not be so, she prayed silently. *Let me make this right.*

The back hallway led to an exit near the cafeteria, and they avoided other partiers in '80s gear as they made their way out. Marisol turned as she reached the door. Teresa watched her with concern. Mari wagged a finger at her.

Once she cleared the door, Russell stepped into her line of vision. His face hadn't lost its clouds yet.

The air outside had cooled as evening changed to night. A bright light shone down over the doorway, illuminating a step down into the wide parking lot in the back of the building where the teachers used to park. The sky overhead embodied that peculiar tone of blue-violet just before the sun truly sank below the horizon, and the evening star hung sparkling overhead near the quarter moon.

Marisol stepped aside, away from the light, into a position more shadowed and less revealing of her emotions. The magic of the evening gone, she stripped off the gloves she had on and shoved them into the pocket of her jacket.

Russell stayed close to the door, the overhead light creating odd shadows on the planes of his face. He started to speak several times but swallowed each aborted attempt with increasing frustration. Finally said, "Are you okay? I'm sorry I didn't stop him sooner. I suspected he might—"

"You knew he intended harm? Did you know that

yesterday?" Even as she said it, she realized that it had to come after the broadcast. *He wouldn't have known what that man's intentions were then.* "Of course. He heard the interview."

"Yes. I think it was a real shock for him. For me, too."

Marisol nodded and rubbed her throbbing arm. "Russell, I didn't know you read the blog. I had no idea before I came back that you and Tiffany weren't still happily married with a houseful of children on Lake Shore Drive. I'd always figured that's what happened." She watched his face for a reaction. "I really *left* here when I left. I didn't follow up with anyone except Analisa, and we really weren't in touch often."

"You hated this town so much?" He frowned and stared out at the sunset. "You hated…me?"

She bit her lip a moment before she replied. "No. That's not what I meant." She crossed her arms, hugging herself for support.

He looked away.

"Rusty, there wasn't anything here for me. It really didn't have to do with you at all. You were history before then." She gave a faint smile to ameliorate any sting of her words. "For better or worse."

He laughed without mirth. "Yeah, we know which of those it turned out to be."

She shook her head. "Regardless, your situation—or this man Stuart's—neither of you had anything to do with the blog. It's hard when you're a woman, alone, with a high school education and no real prospects, nothing other than a baby in your arms, and the father says he's leaving because he can't deal with things. That's why I wrote it. And there are thousands of women, and men too, who are in the same situation."

She stepped farther into the shadows, afraid she'd cry again. She really didn't want him to see her cry any more. "It's like you're standing on a spot the size of a shoebox with a gaping abyss all around you and no way out. It took me three months to get enough nerve to ask for help before we lost our apartment, just to make sure Mark had formula."

"Now look, I never—"

Her voice firmed up and took on an edge, as tears came back to her eyes. "I didn't say you. I said *me*. I don't write for men who have lost their children. I write to encourage women who think they won't survive without a man. I let them know being alone with their child isn't the end of the world. That they won't only survive, but they can thrive, if they get the right attitude. They can have a boy as wonderful as Mark."

She choked on her tears then, and fought for shuddering breath, staring at the ground.

He didn't respond. She wondered if he would just walk off. But he stayed. She cleared her throat, continuing when she thought she could.

"That boy is everything to me. Would I have preferred to raise him in a two-parent home with all the advantages? Of course I would. Would I have preferred his dad to visit and take him places and go to dinner, like you want to do with your boys? Of course. But I didn't have that option. And we survived anyway."

He still didn't respond, standing under the light with his hands in his pockets. The silence drew out so long the empty air called for something else.

"I'm sorry if what I wrote hurt you in any way, but you've got to understand how it is in the blogging world. We write for those who need to read what we have to share. Because it's a world of free speech, people who disagree with what we have to say have the opportunity to do so. I've had my share of trolls, people who just post to be negative and rude. That's what I thought FreeDad91 was doing. I didn't think he was serious. And I never meant to hurt you. I'm sorry if I did."

Marisol looked into his face then, stepping a little forward. There. That's what she had to say, and she'd said it. Russell could accept her apology or not.

Chapter Twelve

Russell was struck speechless.

Marisol had bared her soul to him, the pain of her life, and offered him an apology for what might have been his own mistake in taking what she'd written personally. Any outrage he might have experienced, probably spurred on by Stuart's single-minded hostility, faded away.

The silent woman before him waited for something. What was he to say?

He rubbed his face with one hand, feeling tension build up behind his eyes. A beer would go down real well about now, but they needed some sort of closure to get past this. If she wanted to get past this. If he'd really let himself go, it could have been him Mike kicked out of the dance, not Stuart. He hoped the fact he'd interceded at least made her think of him in a better light. *Right? At least I'm not a total loser.*

"You're right. I'm not mad at you. I'm mad at Tiffany," he said. "I blamed you for the same reason I thought you had taken aim at me. Jerrika Jones was a big bugaboo. Someone I could be mad at, and even say horrible things to, without strings."

A faint smile appeared and then faded off her lips. "I suppose you could still hate me, if it makes you feel better."

"I don't really think that's what I want at all—" He

was interrupted by Marisol's friend Teresa bursting out the door behind him.

"Marisol! Ana just called from the hospital. You've got to go right away. Your son...your father! Come on!"

"What?" Even in the half-light, Russell saw the color drain from Marisol's face. She just stared at Teresa in disbelief.

"What about them? What's happened?"

"You've got to go, *querida*. Come on."

When Marisol still didn't move, Russell reached out and slipped an arm around her shoulder, guiding her toward Teresa. Whatever it was, something in the woman's voice told him it was very serious and they should waste no time. "Marisol, do you have a car?"

"I have a car," Teresa said.

"No, I drove," Marisol murmured, stumbling over the threshold as she went inside.

Russell considered the two of them, one near hysterical and the other in shock. "Better idea. You both ride with me."

Teresa protested, but he put an arm around her shoulders, too. Taller than either of them and able to move them along quickly, he steered them back into the main gym and toward the door.

Mike intercepted him halfway across the floor, the news apparently already reaching him through the police network.

"Does she need a ride? She probably shouldn't drive," he said.

"I've got it, thanks, Mike."

Mike looked to the women for approval. Teresa nodded, since Marisol still seemed as if she hadn't caught up to reality yet. "All right. Let me know if you need anything."

"Will do."

Russell, now focused on getting to the hospital for Marisol's sake, walked her to his car, Teresa following behind. "What's going on?" he asked over his shoulder.

"Analisa didn't say, exactly. Something about a boating accident on the lake."

"Fishing," Marisol murmured as he helped her into the front seat.

"Fishing?"

"Papa was taking Mark fishing tonight. They must have gone out on the lake."

She rocked in the seat a little, arms wrapped tight across her abdomen. Her eyes stared straight ahead, but he didn't think she saw anything in front of her but her son.

He let Teresa in the back seat and slid in behind the wheel. "Hold tight and buckle up, ladies. We're going to leave some rubber." He started the car, floored the gas pedal, and headed downtown.

****

Emergency rooms never seemed to improve much.

Though a frequent guest as a child, Russell hadn't visited one since Jon broke his arm riding his bike at age six. In an emergency room, parents were helpless. You had to count on medical people you've never met. When a father's job was to protect his family and fix things that are broken, it was so hard to stand by and concede those roles to someone else. Memories of that filtered in between the scenes before him as they hurried into the entrance.

Teresa stopped at the triage window and asked for

107

Analisa. "Mark Slade's mother is here," she told the woman seated there.

The nurse stared at their outlandish outfits, no doubt wondering if she'd just slipped back in history twenty years. "I'll call the doctor," she replied. "Please have a seat."

Marisol seemed to shake herself back into this world, and Russell touched her shoulder lightly.

"Mari, whatever you need, I'm here for you. I know if it were my son in there, you'd do the same for me."

Tears in her eyes, she reached out to hug him. "Yes, I would. Thank you so much."

A woman he recognized as Analisa Ramirez, in nurse uniform whites, burst through the swinging door to the treatment area. Her eyebrow went up as she spotted him.

"Mari, come back and the doctor will see you." Her lips pursed together. "Russell, you come, too."

"My father? He is all right?" Marisol asked as they entered through the swinging door. "They were both in the accident? What happened?"

"He was pulled from the water with Mark. He seems to be fine, but very worried." She moved quickly down the hall, her professional oxfords making no sound on the corridor floor. "You'll have to ask them what happened."

The old man sat in the hallway, wrapped in a white blanket, wearing hospital scrubs. Standing in front of him was a man in the uniform of the Crawford County Sheriff's Marine Unit. They were engaged in serious conversation.

Marisol ducked around a lab tech carrying a full

basket of tubes and ran to him, throwing her arms around him before she launched into a barrage of Spanish.

That hospital smell filtering into his nose, making him uncomfortable, Russell turned to ask Analisa for the story, but she had disappeared.

The officer, seeming confused by Marisol's festive clothing, tried to ask Marisol some questions, but she pushed him aside. "Mark?" she asked, and she vanished into the curtained area just behind where her father sat. Russell walked closer, scoured by a hard look in the eyes of Marisol's father.

His English thickly accented, her father said, "You're Asher. The one who broke her heart."

"What?"

The statement delivered such a complete non sequitur it stopped him cold. Russell studied the man, his lined face and worn hands a testament to a life of hard work.

"You broke her heart. How do you have the courage to show your face here?" He pushed himself up out of the chair and tugged the blanket closer around his shoulders before following Marisol inside the curtain.

The words crawled around inside his head and heart like wasps, stinging his conscience. He'd broken her heart? He'd assumed she just moved on. At least, he hadn't given much thought to her feelings. Not at the time.

Seems like we've both done some of that. Time to knock it off.

A nervous twitch confirmed it. He turned to the officer. "So, what happened?"

"Who are you, again? Mr., um, Asher? Is that what

he said?"

"That's right. Russell Asher."

The officer made a note on the pad in his hand. "Looks like a bunch of townie kids were out on a Sea Ray Sundancer, partying for the afternoon and buzzing smaller boats. Mr. Herrera and his grandson were fishing in a thirteen-footer and, when these clowns came by, the wake tipped the boat. Mr. Herrera went in. The boy went after him. Somehow, he got his grandfather back into the boat but couldn't get himself out."

The officer cleared his throat, with a glance into the curtained area. "Several other boaters saw the accident and came over to help. They pulled him out about the time our boat got there."

"Is he going to be all right?" Russell's insides clenched in sympathy for Marisol. He could imagine himself standing next to Jon or Barret's bed in a similar situation, praying for the boy to wake up safely.

"Touch and go, sir," the officer said. "You the boy's father?"

"Me? No." Something inside him added, *I could have been.*

"I see." The officer closed his pad and tucked it in his pocket.

"Any idea who the partiers were?"

"Oh, yeah. They were IDed by half a dozen people. One of the LaMonica girls, Teddy Tomko, the Kearns boys, and the Harsten twins. Boat's registered to Emil Harsten. We'll be talking to all of them. I'll need to talk to Mrs. Slade, when she's had a chance to catch up."

The officer gestured toward the curtain and walked away toward the nurse's desk to ask where he could use his phone.

Russell only half heard everything after the officer said "the Kearns boys." The rising bile at the thought of his sons' involvement became exacerbated by his fury that Jon and Barret were now known as "the Kearns boys."

She'd done it.

Tiffany had succeeded at divorcing not only herself, but her sons, from their unwanted father.

Sick, he walked to the swinging door and back, taking deep breaths to wrestle his self-control into place. He couldn't get overwhelmed by his feelings about Tiffany now. Marisol's son behaved as a hero; he was the boy deserving of Russell's support.

When he'd yanked his focus to the correct spot, he straightened his shoulders and walked back to the curtained area. He rapped on the wall with his knuckles.

Marisol sat on the edge of the bed, holding her unconscious boy's hand as if she'd never let go. Her father hung back at the end of the bed, rosary beads in his hand. Her tear-streaked face turned to him when he knocked.

"May I come in?" he asked.

"What right do you have here?" Mr. Herrera said. "Go away."

"Papa," Marisol scolded gently. "Of course, Russell."

He stepped in, coming to the opposite side of the bed from Marisol. Mr. Herrera snorted in disgust and stalked out. Russell watched him go, ill at ease. "Are you sure?"

"Yes." Marisol turned her attention to her son, her free hand reaching out to caress his cheek. "Mark, *mi'jo*, I'm here. Come back to us."

The boy who beamed so confidently in his senior picture looked younger lying in the white-sheeted hospital bed, under several thick blankets with his luminous eyes—his mother's eyes—closed. Machinery beeped around him, a plastic clip on his left forefinger, an oxygen cannula tucked into his nose. Someone had changed him into hospital pajamas. His wet clothing sat in a large plastic hospital bag on a counter.

Russell studied the machines, trying to remember what he knew about them from watching hours of medical shows on television in his lonely apartment. The one to the right of the head of the bed blinked and beeped with the approximate timing of a heartbeat, reading between seventy and eighty. Acceptable, at least by TV writers' standards. The corner number showed the oxygen reading and registered in the nineties. Also acceptable.

The boy did not need a ventilator and breathed on his own. Surely that signaled something good. But still he didn't wake up, even at his mother's urging.

Russell's hands twitched. He ought to be doing something useful, not intruding on a mother and son's moment of intimacy. The emotion in her voice as she begged him to respond tugged at his heartstrings. Had he ever heard Tiffy speak in that tone to one of their sons? Like she was tied to them by more than what could be humanly seen? Like they were more than just her possessions, little dolls to dress up and put on parade like her shiny new car?

Maybe when they were very young. Certainly he hadn't seen such behavior recently.

Analisa popped in and hugged Marisol, her eyes

scanning the readings on the machine.

"Has the doctor been in?" she asked.

"Not yet," Marisol replied. "*Digame, chica.*"

Analisa glanced over to Russell, gave him a nod and a smile as she let go of her friend.

To Marisol, she said, "Mark wasn't breathing when they got him out of the water, but they revived him on the sheriff's boat. You are very lucky, *querida*. He was in the water less than ten minutes because the other boats were close, so we don't think there will be any neurological damage."

"Neuro what? Isn't that brain damage?" Marisol's eyes widened. "No! He can't have brain damage. He's going to college in September. He's a good boy. He's a good boy!"

Her anxious face turned back to her son, as if willpower alone could revive him.

Russell interjected, "Mari, she said there likely *isn't* any damage."

"Exactly right. The fact it's so late in the summer helps, too, because the lake is warmer. If it had been in the spring, hypothermia might have taken him already. We're keeping him warm, the oxygen he's getting is heated and the IV solution as well, to keep him where we want him to be."

"So what are you saying? He'll be all right, won't he? Tell me he will!"

Analisa's expression didn't change, and Russell's internal BS detectors went off.

She stepped back toward the edge of the curtain. "We think so, Mari. I'll remind the doctor that you're here. I'm sure he'll be in soon to talk with you."

"Anything I can do?" Russell asked Analisa,

feeling at loose ends.

"Just be here. She needs you." A curt nod punctuated her words, and she hurried out.

So Russell stayed.

As the night wore on, the hospital staff transferred Mark upstairs to an intensive care bed, taking no chances. Marisol took that opportunity to speak with her father in the family waiting room while they got Mark settled. Russell, as a non-family member, waited outside, determined to see this through. He watched their animated discussion through the glass, wishing like hell he could numb his growing guilt.

He successfully resisted the temptation to call Tiffy to castigate her for the job she'd done parenting the boys, and the *noblesse oblige* attitude that her family could get away with anything because of their money.

He did, however, call Mike.

"Hey, Mike, it's Rusty," he said when his friend answered.

"Rusty? What the hell time is it?"

"Hmm? Oh, sorry. Probably four a.m." Russell looked around for a clock before he realized he hadn't stopped to think about the time at all. "Sorry, man. I'm still at the hospital."

Mike muttered something unintelligible. "How's the boy? Stasden said it was nip and tuck for awhile."

"He's in ICU," Russell replied, unsure from what Analisa had said whether he really believed Mark would completely recover.

"How are *you*? I gotta tell you, I thought Stuart was going to lose his ass when that woman came in. Good thing you put us on watch. Who woulda thought that anyone could get so excited about some kind of computer stuff?"

Russell's face flushed hot. "Yeah, right? The Internet. Bunch of wackos."

He glanced in through the glass windows in time to see Marisol embrace her father. A nurse came to speak to them, and Marisol disappeared into another room with the nurse. Mr. Herrera, dressed in his street clothes again, glared at him through the glass. Russell nodded to the man, with as much respect as he could display.

"Your deputy said they had a line on who caused this," Russell said. "Any progress there?"

Mike's voice rasped with irritation. "He told you that, did he? Because your boys are involved?"

Russell tried not to snap his response, the audacity of Tiffy's 'name change' still burning him. "He didn't know I was their father. He called them the 'Kearns boys.' Probably just trying to help, not break your confidentiality rules. So? I'm sure you caught up with them."

"Sure did. Not like they didn't leave a trail a mile wide. But they've all lawyered up and are safe in their Lake Shore homes."

Thinking of Marisol's face as she sat with her son, Russell's anger at the rich kids' solution to the problem matched Mike's. "You're going to file charges." It was a statement, not a question.

"Once we know the outcome, I expect we will. We've got reckless endangerment at least, for what happened to the other boaters." Mike cleared his throat, as though his words got stuck there. "Not looking forward to adding negligent homicide. That'll be a bitch to prosecute in this town."

Surely Mark wasn't going to die. The thought

paralyzed Russell. *No. No, it couldn't happen.*

"No one's said that around here. Not yet, at least. Keep me posted, all right?"

"Will do."

Russell sighed as he put his phone back in his pocket. He thought about calling his parents to explain why he stayed out so long, but they'd just assume he was out partying with the reunion crowd. He could tell them all this later.

Especially the part about the boys being involved. He dreaded that most of all.

Mr. Herrera stopped his pacing inside the glass and came out to the corridor. That stubborn wedge still remained between his eyebrows, and no warmth came from his eyes. A good five inches shorter than Russell, he made up for any lack of height with his rebellious attitude. Russell could see where "Jerrika" got that chip on the shoulder.

"What you think you will do for my daughter now, hmm? Take advantage of her while she is distracted and in pain? It's not enough that she run away from here so long ago because of you? That she not be with her family, with her father, all this time because the thought of you drove her away? She. Does. Not. Need. You."

"I know she doesn't. I don't expect anything from her. Not even forgiveness."

Mr. Herrera's stern gaze figuratively bore holes into Russell's face. It compelled him to explain, to justify somehow, even though that look told him nothing he said would make a difference.

"I've made plenty of mistakes in my life, Mr. Herrera. Believe me, I'm learning this every day. It's no excuse to say I didn't mean to hurt Marisol. I was blind.

I thought I knew what I wanted. It's taken twenty years for me to realize I had no idea what was worthwhile, and what was a useless fantasy."

He stepped closer to Marisol's father, prepared, if it came to it, for the man to strike out at him. As a father, he could see how the pain someone caused a child could make that happen. He wasn't sure he didn't deserve it, despite his lack of any bad intention.

"I had no idea she'd even come this weekend. When she wanted to speak to me, I was surprised and grateful. She's done so well for herself..." He shrugged. "I see why you're so proud of her."

The man stared at him, unwilling to back down. "You better not hurt her again," Mr. Herrera grumbled.

"No, sir, I promise."

Small blessings. At least he doesn't know my boys rode in the boat and caused the accident. That guilt reached beyond any apology he could make and would take a long time to set aside.

Marisol's emergence from the ICU saved Russell from any further interpersonal attacks. She'd taken the scarf from her hair and removed the jewelry and the fancy-lapelled jacket she'd worn, now simply dressed in black. Russell thought her loose hair and plain dress suited her so much better.

"How is he?" he asked.

"He's finally sleeping normally," she said, relief flooding her voice. "He's out of the coma."

Chapter Thirteen

Marisol's father gasped, and tears came to his eyes. *"Gracias a Dios! Gran Padre, nosotros gracias!"* He pulled Marisol to him and held her close. *"Gracias, gracias…"*

She clung to him for long seconds, and gently disentangled herself. She'd said the same words, thanking a God she hadn't necessarily believed in all these hard years on her own. For the first time, she truly understood the meaning of the light at the end of the tunnel. After the passage of this dark night, the morning brought a small hope that continued to grow.

"He's going to be all right, Papa. I know it."

The old man stumbled, and she caught him. Although he would never admit weakness, she could see how age crept up on him, stealing away his strong body and health. A twinge of guilt for living too far to care for him personally stung her.

"You need sleep, Papa. I called Ana to come get you. She invited you to stay at her house until Mark is released. It is not far."

"And what will you do? You should sleep, too."

"I can't leave Mark here alone, Papa. I'll stay. I'll call you if there is a change. *Prometo.*"

As if on cue, Analisa stepped off the elevator. She mirrored the same dark circles under her eyes as her friends'.

Marisol smiled and hugged her. "Good news. Mark's out of the coma."

Ana's tired smile was a welcome sight. "Thank God."

"I told Papa you would let him rest at your house." Marisol became very conscious of Russell Asher, waiting off to the side, obviously afraid to intrude. She couldn't believe he waited the whole night, just being supportive. It meant a lot to her. She wanted to be able to tell him.

Her father fussed a bit, but eventually Ana crooked her arm through his and managed him into the elevator. "I'll feed him, too, Mari. Chorizo, eggs, and honey bread like he's never had before. Can I bring you something back?"

Marisol shook her head. "I couldn't eat now. Maybe later."

"*Bueno*. Later. We'll stop back in a couple of hours."

The doors closed behind them, and Marisol breathed a sigh of relief. *But he is not hurt, and Mark will recover.* Her father's protestations of guilt and worry for Mark, plus his worry for her and complaints about the community of West Exeter overwhelmed her. She'd hardly been able to hear herself think.

"What can I get you?" Russell asked.

She studied him. "You can tell me something. Why are you still here?"

"Why?" He looked a little surprised. "I thought you might need something. Coffee? A go-fer? A ride somewhere? A phone?" He shrugged. "A friend?"

His easy smile tugged at her heart the way it had so many years before. Feeling her exhaustion after the long night made her wary of any decisions she might make. But all she really wanted was for someone to hold her and tell her everything would be all right.

"You know what I really need?" she said. "A hug from a friend."

He chuckled, his expression a little amazed. "I can do that."

He held his arms open, and she walked into them, laying her head against his chest. His heart was beating, nearly as fast as hers. He actually trembled a little. She hoped he didn't notice her own nervous flutter twitching all the way to her fingertips.

So many years since they'd stood like this.

Memories crowded in: of her and Russell under the football stadium, at Pamela Johnson's Christmas party, in his Chevy Impala parked along the pier at the lake where the kids used to go for a little privacy and hormonal exploration…

Those memories got a bit graphic.

Marisol pulled away from Russell, taking a step back, not sure she was ready to handle such a detailed visit to the past.

"Did I do something?" His brow furrowed.

"No." She rubbed her forehead, finding the adrenaline of the evening before worn thin since dawn approached. "I should get back to Mark."

He nodded. "You'll want to be there when he wakes up."

Exactly her thought. "Thanks, Russell. I… I appreciate you being here."

He looked down and came over to take her hand. "Marisol, I'm sorry. For what happened earlier. For what happened all those years ago. You know, hindsight is a lot clearer, just like the saying goes. I can't do it over, so there's no use in speculating on what might have been different."

He looked into her eyes, like his own so brown, so dark, so sincere.

"I just want you to know I really admire what you've done with your life. You should be proud of what you've accomplished. Especially with that boy."

He held her hand just a moment longer, then let it slip from his.

Even if words had come to her, the tightness in her throat left her without the breath to say them. She simply turned and walked away.

When her hand closed on the door to the ICU, he said, "I'll be right here if you need something. Just have someone come get me, all right?"

She nodded, still choked up, then went in. *I can't believe he's willing to hang out like that. Who would have expected, of all the people who'd be most interested in her this weekend, it would be Russell Asher?*

She made her way quietly back to the area where they monitored Mark, trying to find encouragement in the noisy machinery instead of fear. She leaned over Mark's bed, running the back of her hand along his forehead, feeling him just warm enough. His breathing came even, no longer wheezing. His skin finally smooth again after the ravages of adolescence, he looked like an angel sleeping.

She kissed his cheek and curled up in the chair next to his bed, sufficiently out of the way so any staff members could get to Mark if they needed to provide treatment. Her eyes burned and would simply not stay open any longer. Just a few minutes, she promised herself. She'd know when Mark woke up. Then her life could begin again.

****

The judge banged his gavel in the courtroom, calling the proceedings to order. Marisol sat with Mark behind the prosecutors' table. Marisol's classmates, Tiffany's best friends, and some of the football players filled the jury box. The noisy room quieted down as the deputy from the sheriff's Marine Unit brought in half a dozen kids, who took seats with several men in expensive suits at the other table.

Most of the room was full of parents and relatives of the young people at the table, all dressed in expensive clothes, lazily fanning themselves with broad paper fans like those from old movie courtrooms, as if they were just marking time.

"Call your witness," the judge ordered from the bench.

One of the suits stood up. "The defense calls Tiffany Kearns."

Marisol gasped and turned to see the slender blonde woman march up the aisle to be sworn in by the clerk. Her designer suit matched exactly the blue of her eyes. She sat in the witness chair like it was a throne.

"Madam, will you state your name?"

"Tiffany Kearns."

"Do you know the defendants in this matter?" The man gestured in a broad sweep to the table at his left.

"I do. My sons and their friends."

Tiffany smiled and waved at the crowd as if riding a homecoming float. Her sons only smirked and lounged in their seats.

"And, madam, should the court find these popular young people guilty of the charges against them?"

"Of course not! This isn't their fault."

Marisol looked to the prosecutors to do something, to interject, but they sat entranced by the lovely Tiffany.

"Well, then, whose fault is it?"

"Russell Asher. It's his blood in them that makes them act bad. Punish him, not them."

The judge banged his gavel. "Bring forth Russell Asher that sentence may be passed upon him!"

Marisol, heart in her throat, rose to her feet as a pair of policemen dragged Russell down the aisle to an open spot in front of the judge. *What were they doing? This wasn't Russell's fault! Tiffany raised them this way, not him.*

The judge stood up and leaned forward to look Russell in the eye. His face showed no mercy, only disgust.

"Russell Asher, this court finds you guilty of attempted murder. You shall be taken from here to the state penitentiary where you shall spend the rest of your so very unnatural life. Take him away!"

"No!" Marisol cried out. "You can't do this! Tiffany Kearns took him away from me once, and I won't let her do it again!"

"Order in this court! Order! Bailiff, remove that woman!" the judge said.

"You can't do this! It isn't right! You can't take him away!"

The bailiff came over and took hold of her shoulder, pulling her away from Mark, while Tiffany smiled and waved in vapid continuity.

Marisol's heart beat so fast she thought it would explode as she reached out to Russell. "You can't—"

With a start, Marisol woke up and yanked away from the hand on her shoulder. "No!"

"Mrs. Slade, it's all right."

The nurse leaning over her seemed perfectly calm, like this happened every day. "I brought you a tray."

"Oh." It took several moments for Marisol to reorient herself to the waking world where things made a little more sense. She looked at the packaged cereal and Styrofoam cups on the table next to the bed without a shred of hunger after what she'd just experienced.

"Bad dreams. Um, thank you." Slowly, she remembered where she was and why she was there and looked over to the bed. Mark was watching her. "Mark?" On her feet in a second, she stepped to the bed and grabbed his hand. He squeezed hers back.

"Well, now, that's good news," the nurse said. She quickly checked his vitals. "I'll call the doctor." She left them alone.

Offering a silent prayer of thanks, Marisol sat on the edge of Mark's bed. "How are you feeling?"

"My throat hurts," Mark said. "Where's Papa? Is he all right?"

"He's fine, *mi'jo*. You saved him." She squeezed his hand. "I'm so proud."

His dear face held a puzzled expression, though he didn't seem surprised he awoke in a hospital. "How long have I been here?"

"Just overnight. They wanted to make sure there was no damage." Her breath caught as she experienced again the panic of her arrival in the emergency room and her fear she'd lose him.

"I can't believe those idiots. They did it on purpose, Mom. They tried to swamp the boat."

"The officer told me when he was here last night, Mark. The law will take care of them, Mark. You weren't the only victims for the day."

"I'm glad they're going after those guys. 'Cause they *were* jerks."

He asked for something to drink, and she shook out a few ice chips from the plastic pitcher on the table. "Suck these until they melt for now. You've got to work up to water, is what they said. Slowly," she urged. "You don't want to upset your stomach."

The doctor came in and sent Marisol outside while he did some testing. When she stepped into the hall, Russell got up from the chair nearest the elevator, knocking his empty paper coffee cup to the floor.

"How is he?"

"He's awake," she said, with a little smile. "And you're still here."

"I told you I'd stay." He bent down and retrieved the cup, then threw it in a nearby wastebasket. His pants were rumpled, and his eyes red from lack of sleep. How sad he'd deprived himself on her account.

Or maybe it wasn't on her account.

"You don't have to do that just because of your boys."

His startled look confirmed he knew what she was talking about. "That has nothing to do with it. I'm all for letting the law run to its fullest extent. Whatever happens, happens. It sounds like they deserve it."

Russell could have blamed Tiffany; certainly Marisol did. But he didn't.

"You know, somewhere they got lost, Mari. I don't

know how they stopped being mine. I must have let them slip away. I don't like what they've become. I'm so sorry they were involved in this incident. I can't believe a child of mine could be so callous and unthinking."

He rubbed his hand across his face.

"When I see a boy like yours, a young man who's working for what he wants, who's a hero, not a punk, I realize all the values I could have instilled in them, if I'd just stood up to her. Just fought a little harder."

She didn't know what to say. He didn't sound like the old Russell Asher at all, the one who was just looking for the best time he could have. The years had been his teachers—and this last incident might have been his final exam.

"So, what are you going to do about it?" she finally asked.

"I guess I'll have to decide if I'm going to court. They need to have at least one parent who holds them accountable for what they do in life." He gave a rueful look. "I can't imagine they're going to like it. But…"

Fighting off the echoes of her earlier dream, Marisol nodded in approval. "Good for you."

"And Marisol—"

"Mrs. Slade?" The doctor interrupted Russell, and Marisol let him.

"Yes?" she asked.

The doctor eyed Russell. Marisol assured him he could speak freely in front of her friend, so he pulled out the chart and looked at his notes.

"Your son looks like he's going to make a complete recovery. You'll have to watch his lungs for the next few weeks. If he develops a cough or inflammation, take him for medical care immediately."

"We have to fly home Monday. Will that be all right?"

"It should be," he reassured her.

"What about his brain?" she asked.

"His brain seems to be fine. Reaction time's good, memory's sharp. He even checked out the nurse's legs." The doctor chuckled. "And Sandra's legs are worth looking at. The boy's got good taste."

Marisol choked back her feminist response and reveled in the good news. "Thank you, Doctor. That's wonderful."

"I'm glad things turned out well. I'll be discharging him soon. You can take him home."

The doctor shook hands with her, then, after an awkward delay, with Russell. He appeared confused about what the man who was not the father was doing there. He retreated with his chart into the unit.

"I'm so happy for you," Russell said. He opened his arms to her again, and she surrendered to the hug. Celebration was the logical conclusion.

"Me, too."

Then Analisa and Marisol's father came off the elevator, and Marisol shared the joyful news. Ana beamed, then went to check in at the nurses' station. Marisol and her father went into the ICU to see Mark. When she looked back from the door, Russell was gone.

Chapter Fourteen

Russell staggered into his parents' house just as his mother was putting on the morning coffee.

"One of those nights, I see," Kate said with a knowing smile.

"You've got no idea." Russell dropped into one of the kitchen chairs and put his head down on his arms on the table.

"Rusty?" Kate came over to him, laid a cool hand on the back of his neck. It comforted him. Now if she could only make his mind stop spinning.

"Honey, what's happened?"

"I spent the night at the hospital," he said. "There was an accident…"

His mother listened to the whole story about Mark and his grandfather, sitting at the table next to him, her hands twisting, fingers rubbing knuckles. "Sweet Lord," she said. "Are they going to charge Jon and Barret?"

"I don't know, Mom. I'd like to hope not. I mean, what parent wants to see their kids go through that? But at the same time, I can't help but think they have to be held responsible for their behavior. What they've done isn't right."

"What about the Herrera girl? Her son, he'll make a full recovery? They're sure?"

"That's what the doctor said."

"Thank God for that." She sat silent for some time, while the coffee pot burbled and spit its way to the completion of the brew cycle. When it finished, she poured them both a cup. She held his out. "If you don't think it will keep you up."

He took it with a tired laugh. "I doubt anything will keep me from sleep at this point."

They drank coffee, the silence stretching between them again. She asked, "So how is Marisol? I always liked her. Better than Tiffany," she added. "Not like you'd have listened to me at the time."

Thinking of Marisol brought a smile to his face. "Besides raising a good son, she's created quite a career for herself."

Explaining to his nontech-oriented mother the concept of a blog and the way it generated income, and even how the Internet worked, took some time, but eventually she seemed to understand how Marisol carved out her own niche in the world.

"I'm glad for her. She deserved better."

Hearing the veiled condemnation from his own mother hurt, but Russell absorbed it into the mishmash of his own troubled feelings. He couldn't deal with it now, not while he hovered on the edge of exhaustion. How had he stayed up all night any time he wanted back in high school? Back in college?

If he'd ever needed evidence he was getting old, this was certainly it.

"I think I'd better crash awhile, Mom. Catch you in a couple of hours, hmm?"

"All right, Rusty."

She stood and hugged him, patting him on the back as if he were a child again, comforting him in the way only she could. "You get some sleep, hear? Then we'll deal with this, all of us together."

"Thanks, Mom. Thanks for being a good parent. I should have appreciated you more often."

He embraced her, feeling gratitude for her slight body and her strong spirit. "Night." He wandered back down the hall and fell into bed without taking off more than his shoes.

****

He woke up halfway through the afternoon, lying in bed for fifteen minutes afterward, just to assimilate all that occurred in the last few days. Nothing unfolded like expected. Least of all the reunion with Marisol Herrera. What a wild ride they'd shared…without any of the bravado he marshaled for the experience.

But now it was Sunday afternoon, and he'd promised to pick up Jon and Barret. Didn't want to miss that, no sir.

He bailed out of bed and hit the shower. He must look at least as good as Paul Dupont if he wanted to get in the door of the Kearns house. After a thorough scrub, he put on the aftershave Tiffy always liked—couldn't hurt, right?—and dressed in his sharpest slacks and shirt.

The drive over, cloudy and gray, matched his mood. He thought about interacting with sons callous enough to dump a grandfather and grandson into the lake without taking a moment away from their partying.

He anticipated the battle Jon threatened on Friday and rehearsed his intended argument about why spending time with people other than the twins and Teddy Tomko—bad influences all—would be a great idea. Why coming to Cleveland once in a while other than during the Browns' season would expand their horizons. Why their father should matter. Why a father mattered at all.

Admiring the landscaped lawn as he walked under the brick portico, he considered the effect of access to large amounts of money on one's moral compass. He'd wanted that money once, but that desire hadn't served him or the boys very well. He expected Tiffy hadn't been well served either, despite her carefully-maintained appearance. Most of that was probably fake, too.

He rang the bell.

Seconds ticked by before the uniformed maid opened the heavy wooden door. Her eyes opened a little wider as she recognized the visitor, and she did not smile. "What is your business here, sir?"

Russell tried to look casual, a finger looped into the top of his pocket. "I'm here to pick up my sons."

"They're not seeing guests today, sir."

She started to close the door. He stepped in with his shoulder and blocked it.

"They'll see *me*."

"Sir, I've been instructed to call law enforcement if you come inside this house," the young woman said. Her alarmed expression deepened, and she looked over her shoulder.

"Just call my sons," Russell said firmly.

A voice came from behind the maid. "That will be all, Pamela."

The maid let go of the door handle like it was ablaze and ducked away into a back hall.

Russell stepped all the way inside. The atmosphere showcased a classic décor, antiques, and expensive rugs providing a blush of color against stark white walls.

"Ah, that Kearns hospitality. So legendary, so cold as ice." He studied Tiffany, her face hard like a sculpture. For all he knew, her face could have been "done" or at least adjusted with some sort of preservative shots.

"The boys are indisposed, Russell. They won't be visiting with you today."

"Attempted murder is rough on a conscience, I'd expect. If they even have one."

"Murder?" Tiffany's brow furrowed. Not entirely frozen by injected botulism, then. How nice for her. "What are you talking about?"

"Come on, Tiff. You've got your pet lawyers working on it already, I'm sure. You and the other walking checkbooks think you'll buy your way out of criminal charges for what our children did to Marisol's father, her son, and the other people on the lake yesterday."

"I don't 'think' we'll handle it. I know it's under control. Aren't you happy, Russell, that our sons won't have to be bothered with a nasty criminal matter to ruin their chances at a perfect life? Could you get that for them, Russell?"

Her sapphire eyes looked at him, dissected him as if he were something scraped off the bottom of her shoe.

"I didn't think so."

Russell's outrage built till he nearly burst. "You can't buy them out of this!"

Her smile appeared picture-posed, without emotion. "I already have. My lawyer paid a call on your ex-girlfriend this afternoon to extend an offer of financial security that poor little migrant girl could never have hoped to achieve in her miserable life. She'll head back to her little hole in the ground with enough money to keep her in tortillas for years to come."

Stunned at the chutzpah of a woman he thought he knew, Russell shook his head. "She'd never take it."

"I assure you, she did. So our business for today is concluded. Good day." She gestured toward the door.

"Tiffy, you can't keep me from the boys. They need a father."

"They have all the family they need." She crossed to the bottom of the slightly curving stairway that led to the open hallway of the second floor and picked up the cordless phone. "Now, either you leave voluntarily, or I will call the police to report an intruder in our happy home."

Russell caught movement out of the corner of his eye on the second floor landing. Jon and Barret stood there, looking down on him, in every sense of the words.

Tiffany started to dial the phone, and Russell held up a hand.

"Look, Tiffy. Fine. You win for today. They don't want to see me, and frankly, I'm very disappointed in them. Give me five minutes, I'll say goodbye, and the next time we see each other, it will be in court. All right?"

He only half bluffed.

She studied him, her expression showing doubt in his sincerity, but she hesitated and put down the phone. She glanced up at the boys but didn't call them down.

"You boys want to do this eye to eye like men?"

Russell asked them.

They didn't move. Barret looked at his mother, but his feet stayed firmly planted on the Persian rug runner.

"I didn't think you had the guts." Russell sighed. "You think your mother's going to always be able to get you out of trouble, no matter what you do. I hope for your sake, then, you decide to make good choices."

He eyed them intently. Jon didn't flinch, but Barret looked away again, to his mother, seeking support.

"I just want you to know that I'm here for you, too. I may not be able to buy you what your mother can, or pay off people you hurt, but I can help you be better men. You *need* to be good men in this life. I believe that so strongly that I'm willing to take this matter before a judge and show him why you need me."

Russell's throat closed up, and he pinched his leg through the lining of his pocket to keep himself from showing the pain and regret flooding over him. He was going to get through this. He was.

He coughed to loosen his voice. "You boys know where I live, and you know my email and my phone number. I'll be waiting to hear from you."

A deep breath escaping him as he finished, he caught Tiffy's gloating face and resisted the urge to walk over and slap it off her. A final glance upward showed Jon still giving out the company line, but Barret looked a little shaken. Maybe he could be saved.

Maybe not.

Keeping his shoulders straight and his head high, he turned and walked out of the house.

He almost made it to the car before the door to the house burst open. Barret stood there on the threshold, glancing back into the house over his shoulder, guilt written on his face. "Dad? Tell that boy I'm sorry, will you?"

Russell heard Tiffany screech from inside, and he gave his son a smile. "You bet I will, Barret." He made a gesture with his hand next to his ear, like a phone. *Call me*, he mouthed before Tiffany yanked the boy back inside and slammed the door.

The tiniest window of hope opening before him, choked him up again. He climbed in the car, but only got two blocks before his vision blurred so badly with tears he had to pull over and let the sorrow take him.

He wiped his face on his sleeve when he finally got control, a shuddering breath wrapping his release. He'd done what he needed to do, and he'd follow through.

Oddly enough, he could almost hear Jerrika Jones approving his actions. He stood up to the Kearns machine and tossed them the ball, not letting them just kick him.

But Tiffany's charge that Marisol got bought off so easily bothered the hell out of him. He knew she wasn't rich, or even well off. Sure, she could use the money, especially with her boy going off to school. What he knew of Marisol and her family, though, indicated her moral fiber wouldn't let her cave in, especially to a family who nearly killed her father and son.

He pulled out his cell and did a people search, looking for a number for Analisa Ramirez. Before Marisol left town, he must know what kind of person she was, and what that meant for both their futures.

Chapter Fifteen

While Ana got ready for work, Marisol cleaned up their lunch dishes. She and Mark would soon drive down to her father's to stay till their Monday afternoon flight. This weekend in West Exeter, never a particularly kind place to her, confirmed she'd made the right decision to leave.

Except for Russell Asher.

She'd come back to town with a chip on her shoulder, something to prove to the man who'd walked away from her, and she'd done it.

At the same time, they reconnected. Maybe they could begin again, with more maturity and a knowledge of what truly mattered in life.

Impossible.

She entertained no intention of staying around the area. The climate in nearby Cleveland, especially the east suburbs, wasn't any kinder in winter than in West Exeter, perhaps less so. And despite the presence of Ana, Teresa, and a few others, the town certainly hadn't welcomed her back. Maybe she didn't have the wealth of the Kearns family. Maybe she didn't want to think how those people had gotten that wealth in the first place, considering the example of their current conduct.

Mark rested on the sofa in the living room and struggled to his feet to answer a knock at the door. He came to the kitchen with an odd look on his face.

"Mom, it's for you."

"Who is it?"

"Says he's a lawyer representing Tiffany Kearns."

Her temper simmered, ready to hit a boil. How dare he come here?

She became even more outraged when he offered her five thousand dollars to waive prosecution of Jon and Barret Kearns. He promised if she was willing to do the same for the other families, she'd receive an even bigger "windfall."

"So how much is that exactly?" she asked in amazement. "Twenty-five hundred for each of your clients' children? Fifteen thousand dollars if I'll just go home and be quiet?"

The dark-suited man nodded and smiled, an oily smile better suited to a con man than a member of a profession Marisol thought was supposed to uphold ethics and the laws.

"We're all grateful, of course, that your son seems to have received no permanent injury." He nodded at Mark, who watched him with suspicion from Ana's kitchen table. "This would be in the way of—"

"An apology?" she snapped.

"Not exactly. Just compensation for any inconvenience that might have been caused. If you'll just sign this release, I have a check here for you."

He drew a blue check from his briefcase and showed it to her. Her name marked the "Pay to" line, and the amount thereon was $5,000.

Her stomach seemed to leap from its usual place as she pondered what to do. Granted, she did have Mark back, safe and well from all accounts. That check alone could get them through months of expenses at home, or provide her with a car to use after Mark had gone to school, or…

And he'd promised more.

A lot more.

She stared at the check but didn't reach to take it. He stepped closer, still holding it out.

If there remained any hope of rekindling a relationship with Russell Asher, what would happen if she and Mark witnessed against his sons in a court proceeding? She knew this wasn't his fault and didn't suspect him in this brash attempt at bribery. But forcing his boys, and him, through the embarrassment of a public trial, wouldn't that strain any chance they had?

Looking at the situation from a more practical position, could she in good conscience turn this down? Mark needed so much for school in the fall. She chewed her lip, the discomfort it caused offsetting the nausea of indecision.

The hired gun started to look uncomfortable and waved the check at her. "Well, Mrs. Slade, are you taking the deal or aren't you? Time is money. The clock's running out on this opportunity."

What would Jerrika do? Marisol wondered. She considered those options, looked the man in the eye, and took the check.

"Time is money? Is money time?" She looked down at the paper in her hands. "Could this really pay me for the time I spent last night not knowing if my boy was going to live? Had your clients even stopped drinking and partying by that time? By four o'clock? By six?"

She eyed him, feeling hostility bubble up inside. "How much is agony worth, in terms of by-the-hour, sir? Does that get a premium? How about heartbreak? What do you get for that? Is that more or less per hour than just annoyance?"

He didn't even look her in the eye. His gaze stayed locked on the check as he fumbled in his pocket for a pen for her to sign the release.

"I'm sure you'll feel better about all this in a few days," he said, holding out the release.

"I'm sure I'll feel better about it right now."

Marisol held up the check and ripped it in half, then ripped the pieces in half, and ripped those in half. She reached for his hand and shredded the pieces into it. "Get out of here. Those kids are going to jail, all of them, and I hope it's soon! Get out!"

The lawyer's face got red, and he started to say something, but her fixed angry stare apparently convinced him she meant what she said. He slammed his briefcase shut and turned his back on her, heading out the door.

Stunned silence followed his hasty exit, interrupted at last by the clapping of Mark's hands and his delighted laughter.

"You go, Mom! Talk about Slam Dunk, Game Over. You're awesome!"

He came over and hugged her, bringing tears to her eyes.

"I know how hard that was, *mamacita*. With me going to school and all, we could use the cash. But it's blood money. What if something worse had happened?" He studied her tear-streaked face. "They have to be taught the lessons you've always taught me. Responsibility and care for others. If their parents can't teach them, the courts will."

She shook her head and stepped back, smoothing her shirt, nerves making her hands tremble. "I doubt the courts will even see this. But you're right. We don't have to be part of it."

"Awesome," he said again with his crooked grin, as he grabbed their suitcases to carry out to the car.

****

They'd driven to her father's modest apartment on a maple-lined street in Mercer to stay till their flights Monday afternoon. Papa still obsessed over the accident, feeling responsible for taking Mark out on the lake. Both Marisol and Mark assured him repeatedly it wasn't his fault.

"Fishing is good for a man. It's what you always say, Papa." Marisol hugged him until he stopped protesting.

Mark added, "I enjoyed it, Papa. Well, right up till the swimming in the lake part." He grinned in the way only he could.

Marisol watched him, this son who gave her moments of awe and wonder daily. He was the best thing that had ever happened to her. Her wonderful father, too. He didn't care about Mark's dark skin or how much money Marisol made, or even the fact she could be famous someday. He was just the man who had loved her since the day she was born, for only what she'd come with.

Blessed with two such men in her life, how could she ask for anything more?

All the same, she couldn't get Russell out of her mind.

She could have called him.

She could have emailed him.

She could have even posted on his blog. Jerrika knew where to find it.

But could she count on what she'd lost so long ago? Even though they'd connected again, now away from his presence, his compelling presence, she began to re-establish the distance between them that had protected her all these years.

They'd experienced the opportunity to forgive each other. Maybe that was enough.

She let that thought carry her through the rest of Sunday as she, her father, and her son cooked together, sang together, and spent the evening leafing through old family photo albums. The journey served as a new experience for Mark, as he discovered his roots, and a welcome reminder for Marisol.

Some of the albums from her high school years showed her as the skinny kid of yore, all legs and eyes, and Mark got his digs in. Several pictures had been removed from the pages. Her calculation of time frame and her father's guttural mutters led her to believe those pictures must have showed Marisol and Russell in happier days.

When they went to bed that night, Mark hugged her tenderly, in a way that brought tears to her eyes. "Thanks for bringing me this weekend, Mom," he said. "It's been really life-changing for me in a lot of ways."

"Me, too, *mi'jo*. I've learned a lot about myself."

He hesitated, fidgeting in his bare feet on the hardwood floor. "Are you going to see him again, Mama?"

"Who? Russell?" Her face flushed. "I don't know, Mark. Some days my life is complicated enough."

"You've spent all this time taking care of me, I

know. But I'm grown now. I'll be going off to school." He looked down at her, his dark eyes shining with an echo of her tears. "You deserve some happiness for yourself."

"Markie, I don't need your permission."

He winked at her. "Maybe not. But you've got it. Get wild, woman."

"Get some sleep," she mock-scolded. "Long day tomorrow getting home."

She waited till he went into her father's room to share Papa's double bed, and she retreated to her mother's old sewing room to sleep on her worn upholstered pink loveseat.

****

Exhausted after the hospital ordeal, and feeling safe in her father's house, she slept so late the next day Mark needed to wake her barely in time to meet the airlines' recommended preboarding time for Pittsburgh.

Her father shoved a brown-bag lunch in her hand and kissed her roughly on the cheek as she went out the door.

"Call when you get home!" he called. "You're doing a great job with that boy. He's a good boy."

Delighted, she waved as she hurried out to the rental car, where Mark already waited in the driver's seat. He'd insisted. "Thank you, Papa. Thanks for keeping him."

He stood on his front step while they backed out of his short driveway and waited as they drove down the street of his small neighborhood. Even when they turned the corner at the end of the block, he stood there, small and so much older than she remembered. *Maybe even older just this weekend.*

Emotion welled up in her as she left him, along with the feeling she might not see him again. She'd asked him to come to live with them in Florida, but he'd insisted he was too old to make such a change at this point. He loved his place, knew his neighbors and his little neighborhood shops, and he would probably die there.

Could she really leave him alone?

Guilt ran through her as she let Mark drive the two hours to the airport, as she considered her options again.

Perceptive as always, her son seemed to echo her thoughts.

"Papa seems lonely, doesn't he?"

"I asked him to come stay with us." A defensive edge sprang to attention like a lizard's startled ruff into her voice. "He could have your room, he could play dominoes with the Cubans down at the park. But he won't come."

Mark digested that for a moment.

"So. Which of you is Mahomet, and which is the mountain, hmm?"

Chapter Sixteen

He must get to the airport by three.

If he didn't, he knew he'd regret it the rest of his life.

Analisa gloated like a satisfied matchmaker or fairy godmother when she'd finally called Russell back. "You're looking for her, aren't you? You realized you were a big *jerk* and you should have been with her, right?"

Put off that she saw through his motive so clearly, he was glad as hell she couldn't see the heat of embarrassment flush through his skin.

"If it gets me her number faster."

Analisa laughed, something in her amusement telling him she knew just what was going on. "She's not even here, hon. She went to her father's last night and by now, she's probably on her way to the airport."

No!

Had he said that aloud? He didn't think so. He hoped not. He took a deep breath, trying to be calm. "Do you know if someone came to see her? A legal type?"

Analisa snorted in disgust. "That pig. Sure, he came."

He was almost afraid to ask. "What... what happened?"

"Ha! She sent the fool packing. As if Miss Priss

Tiffany could buy the life of that boy." A pause and little catch of breath showed her sudden realization she spoke with the father of those boys. "I mean—"

"No worries with me, Analisa. She did the right thing. Those boys will get what's coming to them, if I have to see it through myself."

"I always knew your heart was in the right place. Someplace." She laughed again, and Russell bathed in her approval.

"Where's she flying out of?"

"Pittsburgh." Her amusement continued. "Maaaaaybe you should see if you can catch her before she flies away."

He debated showering her with sarcasm, chose gratitude instead. "Thanks. You're a lifesaver."

Within fifteen minutes, he'd packed his cases, bid his father goodbye, and nearly made it out the door before his mother caught his sleeve and screeched him to a stop.

They'd already talked about how he'd handled Tiffany and the boys. What else could she want?

"Mama, I've got to run. Really," he insisted.

She studied his face. "I can see you're on a mission, son. I'm just wondering what it is."

"Mama…"

She ignored his exasperation. "I pray the mission involves a woman who needs you. Who you need, too."

Something in his eyes must have given him away, because she broke into a fond smile. She hugged him close.

"Don't you let her get away this time, Rusty," she said.

"I won't, Mama, if you ever let *go*!"

Her delighted laugh following him down the stairs, he hurried across to his car and tossed the suitcases in the passenger seat, not even taking time to open the trunk. Years had slipped through his fingers already. He couldn't bear to waste another second.

He'd made this trip along the highway hundreds of times over the years. Home from holidays. Home from events. Back from vacations. He couldn't really remember many other occasions when he headed on this road *toward* something instead of just retreating into his barren life.

If he had a chance.

If he could convince her.

If what he'd read in her hadn't been induced by the strange circumstances of the weekend.

If...

His eye out for speed traps, he tucked the Lexus in behind a convoy of semi truckers and let his foot grow heavy on the accelerator. Whitesnake came on the rock and roll channel he'd dialed into, and the plaintive guitar and harsh drumbeat of "Is This Love?" filled the car. He let the lyrics tear his ego to shreds as he applied them to his life as it stood, and prayed he'd get to the airport in time.

****

Marisol let Mark handle all the luggage transactions at the curb after they dropped off the rental car. She exhibited no patience at all for the security rigmarole. Even her son got a little fed up with the questions and complaints.

Finally they headed into the terminal.

Marisol's big purse held her netbook, along with a camera she'd brought along and used only to take pictures of the four of them at the Friday night dinner. Mark carried his game device in his pocket. But they both agreed they would most likely just sleep for the three hours back. Heavy-duty weekend, for sure.

They waited their turn at the security checkpoint as impatiently as the other passengers. Her bag just entered the X-ray scanner when she heard her name paged over the airport announcement system.

"Mom?" Mark turned to her. "You think there's a problem with Papa?"

"I don't know." She stepped out of line and asked for her bag back, knowing this likely opened her to harsher scrutiny the next time she passed through. "That was me," she said, pointing up toward the speaker as if they would take notice. But no one paid attention. They just moved on to wand the next person in line.

"Where did it say to go?" she asked Mark as they walked away from the concourse, against the flow of pedestrian traffic.

"I think the airline ticket counter."

He walked in front of her, helping open a path through the crowd. "This way."

The walk seemed interminable, but finally they came into a more open space and could walk naturally. The loud buzz of human babble faded, and the music came into focus. Whitney Houston's "Saving All My Love For You."

God.

How many nights had Marisol played that song over and over, crying into her pillow after she'd lost Russell to that woman?

She'd never be able to count.

The words echoed around in her head even after the song finished. Then she saw him. She froze in place.

He saw her at the same time.

"Marisol! Thank God." Russell hurried over to her, looking more like an awkward teenager than a grown man. "I didn't want to miss you."

"Russell, what do you want?" she asked, half denying the physical evidence that he was even here. What did he think he was doing?

Maybe he was coming to beg for the futures of his sons.

The negative thought spiraled through her mind. She couldn't help it. She'd have tried whatever it took to save her son, too.

"You left your white horse at home," Mark said.

Both Russell and Marisol gave him an odd look and looked back at each other.

"White horse?" Marisol asked.

"Not that I think you need s-saving," Russell said quickly, tripping over his words.

"I don't."

What was he up to?

Russell fidgeted, rocking his weight onto the balls of his feet, then onto his heels. He coughed awkwardly. "Analisa told me you turned down Tiffany's money."

His eyes gave her no clue where he was going.

"That's right. I'm... I'm sorry about the boys, but—"

"No!" he answered quickly. "Don't be." He turned to Mark. "I wish my boys were more like you. I'm so glad you didn't... I mean..."

"Thanks." Mark seemed unsure for a moment

before asking Russell, "So why did you come, then? Mama said you lived in Cleveland, so I know you're not catching a flight here. You clearly came after her. And it's not to pay her off, like your ex did. You have no need to find me, so you're looking for my mother. You want to tell her something. Right?"

Nonplussed, Russell's jaw dropped a little. "I…ah. Yeah. Yeah, that's it."

Mark turned to Marisol. "Look, I know this isn't really my business, but you two are acting like…well, like teenagers. Just say what you need to say, Russell. And Mama, you listen, because I know you need to hear it. And then we have to go catch a plane before it leaves." He crossed his arms and eyed them.

Practically watching her boy grow up before her eyes, Marisol blushed and looked at Russell. "So what did you want to say?"

Russell's lips parted as if he was going to speak, but instead glanced at Mark. "This is adult business," he said, and he took Marisol's arm gently and pulled her aside. Mark snickered and turned away, perhaps to give them privacy.

"He's got a chip on his shoulder, doesn't he? I wonder where he gets it?" Russell smiled at her.

"Yeah. I wonder."

She studied his face, familiar again after all those years. Those eyes had warmed her through the Pennsylvania chill, the lips she'd kissed a hundred times. Her self-arguments aside, something in her thrilled at the reconnection, even with all the roadbumps of the past few days.

"What is it you wanted to say, Russ?"

"Mari…" He took a deep breath and paused.

149

She considered how funny it was they'd both reverted to diminutives. Not funny ha-ha. Funny peculiar. Or funny happy. Or…

Without warning, he leaned down and kissed her.

Right. She was thinking too much.

She let go of any objections, relived the sensations, revisited Whitney's sentiments. She'd saved her love for him, even while married to Kirby. She'd never cared for Mark's father the way she'd loved Russell Asher.

What if he could have been Mark's father?

Was it too late?

The warmth that ran through her at his touch short-circuited her constant need to analyze. For once, she just let herself enjoy, without worrying about consequences.

Some time later, she didn't know how long, they broke apart. Announcements still came from the speaker overhead. People still hurried by, their carry-ons strapped to their shoulders. Uniformed crew walked past on the way to their outbound flights.

But the world had changed.

She knew she was loved.

"Mom?"

Mark tapped his watch, and she knew he was right. They couldn't stay.

"We've got to catch a p-plane," she stammered, seeing the same reaction in Rusty's face.

"I know," he said. But he didn't let go of her.

"What are we going to do?"

"I've got three weeks' vacation," he said. "I could come down. You could come back up. We have Internet here, you know. Your blog can come from anywhere."

"I… I know." This was impossible.

"Mom? Plane?" More impatient this time.

"I'm coming, Mark." She slid reluctantly out of Russell's arms. "I'll email you."

"You have a webcam?" he asked, just as reluctantly letting her go.

"I don't." Who could afford that?

"I'll buy her one!" Mark was at his limit now. "You can play Romeo and Juliet later. Now I've got to get home to get ready for school, okay?" He took the strap of Marisol's bag in hand and tugged on it. "*Por favor, Mamacita.*"

"*Bueno, mi'jo. Ya venga.*" With an indulgent smile, she said, "You see how it is?"

Russell nodded. "I see. I'll email you my instant messenger at least. I want to hear that you got home safely."

"I'd like that." Her smile widened till it pulled at her face.

Mark stepped forward and reached out to shake Russell's hand. "I hope I'll see more of you."

Russell looked delighted and smiled. "I'd like that."

"Now we have to go." Mark started to drag Marisol away. "Okay. Goodbye. Goodbye. See ya. *Adios. Hasta la vista*, babee."

Marisol waved and nearly tripped as she went backward, wanting to keep Russell in sight till she turned the corner to the security gate. He waved too, his smile surely as broad as her own.

When they moved past the wall, she turned to walk forward. "You crazy boy. How did you learn so much about people?" she asked Mark.

"I know about love, Mama."

They became separated a few moments while they went through the machines and their bags were scanned. They'd gone through a different line, so no one remembered her earlier impatience.

Once reunited, they walked with brisk steps down the concourse toward their gate and waiting plane. The blue carpet seemed to stretch endlessly, and she wished for a moving sidewalk like they'd seen in Chicago.

"So you know about love, do you?"

"Sure." He smirked at her. "Why do you think I chose Florida State instead of Miami?"

Startled, she stopped walking. "Why?"

"'Cause Kiko's going there."

"What?" Her mouth fell open. "I thought it was because of the forensics program!"

"Come on." He grabbed her hand and pulled her forward. "The program's fine. It's just I know when feelings are that strong, you shouldn't ignore them."

They reached the gate and waited in line for their ticket check.

Marisol didn't know how to respond. No question such strong feelings forged her with Russell. The magnetism pulling at her when she stood close enough to look in his eyes, the electricity of that kiss...

"You're right, *mi'jo*. Maybe there's something in the future for Russell and me. We'll just have to take our time and find out, right?"

"Of course, right!"

The ticket agent hardly noticed them as she ran her gaze over their paperwork and gestured to the boarding door. "Have a nice day," she murmured without emotion while she reached for the next passenger's ticket.

As Marisol followed her son down the long hall of the airbridge, she heard him chuckling over his shoulder. "What?" she asked.

"I was just thinking about that saying about how as kids get older, their parents get smarter? I don't know about that. I mean, how many hints did you need? I practically had to shove you into his arms. Geez…"

She didn't answer him. She just let him glory in his triumphant moment. He'd earned it. The end result remained the same. Her chance at the love of her life had come around a second time. This time she wasn't allowing anyone to get in her way, even if it took Jerrika Jones to firm up Marisol's determination.

After all, Jerrika had brought them together again.

She took her seat and looked out the window at the sunlit skies, grateful for Jerrika, for Russell, and for Mark. Each brought her different opportunities, and she resolutely vowed not to make her prior mistakes again. She could be patient, she could wait a little longer. She'd take it slowly this time, the wisdom of maturity, a glass both she and Russell could use to see their path ahead. If they worked it just right, the fantasy she'd hardly dared dream all these years now hovered on her horizon.

"Ready to take off, Mom?" Mark asked.

"So very ready, Mark. Clear flying from here on out."

She smiled as she relaxed in the seat and the plane pulled away from the terminal. Clear flying now, on course for her dream at last.

Epilogue

A post from the *Parenting Apart or Together* blog, dated July 2011:

Good morning, friends! Marisol here. I can't believe it's been nearly six months since Rusty moved to Ocala. We've talked so much in the pages of this blog about how to be a good parent, and how important it is to keep trying, even in the face of life's obstacles.

Many of you have shared with us your stories of triumph, how you overcame disabilities, addictions, and even the tragedies of the court system to be able to give your children the time and attention they need from you. Each of you is an inspiration to us, and to the other readers of the blog, and I encourage you to keep sending them in.

Thank you for all the support you've given Rusty in his own court battle for his sons. I'm pleased to say the judge allowed Barret to visit his father this summer for the very first time, and we shared a delightful month with him. His older brother chose not to come, which did make Rusty sad, but he is grateful for Barret's time here.

Even Mark has given his full approval to this new, different family we have. He's out with Barret this afternoon fishing at the lake. What a great experience for him, to be a big brother at last! Rusty says Barret couldn't have a finer example of what kind of man he should be. I'd say Barret has two great men to model himself after, and I couldn't be prouder that both of them are part of my life.

Saturday's post this week will be by Rusty, when he shares some of the secrets which helped him reconnect with his long-absent son. So come back and join us during your weekend.

Have a great week, and as always, remember the connection between you and your child goes right down to the microscopic parts we can't even see. Don't let them slip away—be there for them, whatever it takes!

A word about the author…

Alana Lorens dreamed for many years of finding her very own knight on a white steed, or perhaps being one herself. Instead she settles for flights of fancy, inspired excursions into fictional places with fascinating companions from her imagination that she likes to share with others. She has been a published writer for over thirty years, including seven years as a reporter and editor at a newspaper in Homestead, Florida. Her list of publications is eclectic, from science fiction to romance to horror, from tech reporting to television reviews, and a blog about autism, a journey she shares with other parents of special needs children. Alana has retired from her life as a family law attorney, and now lives as a post-modern hippie in Asheville, North Carolina. www.alana-lorens.com

Thank you for purchasing
this publication of The Wild Rose Press, Inc.

For questions or more information
contact us at
info@thewildrosepress.com.

The Wild Rose Press, Inc.
www.thewildrosepress.com